Sheriff of Green Coulee

Jack Griffin had only taken on the job of deputy sheriff to help out ageing Sheriff Tom Mortimer who had just lost his previous deputy. Now Jack was under orders to bring Ern Spiceland back to Green Coulee to answer charges of rustling. What he hadn't expected was Ern attacking him and leaving him unconscious in the Texas Panhandle.

But worse was to come for when Jack finally hit town again, intending to turn in his badge, he was soon to find the sheriff dying of lead poisoning just like his old deputy. Jack's dander was up and he was determined to bring the killer to justice and expose the man behind all the trouble on the range.

Could he stay off Boot Hill long enough though?

Sheriff of Green Coulee

COLT MAHONE

A Black Horse Western

ROBERT HALE · LONDON

ISBN 0 7090 7184 1

Robert Hale Limited
Clerkenwell House
Clerkenwell Green
London EC1R 0HT

Typeset by
Derek Doyle & Associates, Liverpool.
Printed and bound in Great Britain by
Antony Rowe Limited, Wiltshire.

1

Murder in Green Coulee

Hot and gritty sand choked his mouth. With his return to consciousness, his numbed mind tried to flash orders to his body. With his arms, he pushed himself up. Spitting, shaking his head, he stared at the sand.

He forced his brain to think. He knew he was not wounded. He could see his stetson on the ground before him, and he could feel the throb-throb of his head. He touched his head and felt sticky blood.

He reached for his hat and put it on slowly. He looked around and uttered a short, grim laugh.

He felt pretty sure he would not see Ern Spiceland! He remembered the hot, angry words Ern had flung at him, and then the fight. Ern had lashed out with his fists.

Jack Griffin realised he had been punched clean off his horse and had probably struck his head on a rock! He did not know how long he had been out, but probably Ern Spiceland had ridden off the moment he fell.

The fight had been unexpected. Jack had been take by surprise. One moment they had been exchanging caustic remarks, and then Ern's hot anger had spilled over.

Ten yards away Jack's horse was ground hitched, nosing for green grass amid the thorn and sand.

Jack climbed into the saddle, held the reins loosely and spurred the animal. The land around him was pretty arid even for the Texas Panhandle. If a man wanted shade, he would have to sit under his horse's belly.

He had been riding off the trails with Ern Spiceland, making for the town of Green Coulee. Early that morning Jack had ridden out of town on his hired horse and had travelled over to Ern's ranch Then, in the mid-day heat, they had set off together for Green Coulee.

Just that morning Jack had volunteered as deputy sheriff of the cow town. He had offered his services when he heard that Sam Brant, the previous deputy, had been shot by an outlaw. He had taken the job on the understanding that he could quit when he decided to buy a ranch. Immediately, Jack had been sent out to bring Ern Spiceland back to the town for questioning.

'Jest go git thet ornery Ern Spiceland,' Tom Mortimer, rugged old sheriff of the cow town, had grunted. 'I'll tell yuh more about the charge later. I kin tell yuh this – he's got cows on thet spread o' his thet don't belong to him, so I'm told.'

For many miles the tree-less, water-less plain belonged to the big Bar-K ranch. And at the end of the plain, here the hills lifted slowly and the grass grew sparsely between sand and shale, lay Ern's poor ranch. Ern had filed claim to a Round-O brand, and his cattle were branded thus.

Ern was a bright-eyed, swarthy hombre who said little to anyone when he came to town. Most men liked him.

Jack had not seen any rustled cattle on the Round-O, but there was nothing conclusive about that. The longhorns could be hidden in the foothills. He had not bothered to look. He had had orders to bring Ern Spiceland back to Green Coulee and that only. There was nothing else he had to do.

Ern had gone along, without advancing any views or objection. It seemed queer. But he had saddled his big roan and left with Jack Griffin. He and Jack had met more than once in Green Coulee's saloons and had been friends.

Jack rowelled his hired horse and found the trail leading to town. Green Coulee was a blur on the horizon. All around the territory was flat, with mesquite and catsclaw. He came across a few Bar-K cattle, and those scraggy, leery longhorns eyed him suspiciously. It would be round-up time in a few weeks. Maybe there was some connection here between Tom Mortimer's instructions and Ern Spiceland's behaviour.

Now he was returning without his man.

But more than that, he figured he would be returning his deputy sheriff's badge to Tom Mortimer. He had taken on the job only because Sam Brant lay on a bed in the back of the sheriff's office – and Sam, who had been the deputy sheriff, was severely wounded. He had been shot by Mike Capstaff.

Mike was an outlaw. Sam Brant had found him in the Red Pine saloon. But Sam had found a gun-fight, and he had got the worst part of it. Then Capstaff had ridden out of town, shaking off a half-hearted pursuit.

Green Coulee was a roaring cow town, with saloons, honky-tonks and cattle corrals. And there were things going on in Green Coulee which Jack Griffin did not like.

But Jack had recently returned to the county. He had spent three years as a bounty hunter, chasing bad-men for the sake of the price on their heads. He had worn two guns most of those three years – and slept with them. Then he had returned to Green Coulee, the town he had known as a boy.

He had been back in Green Coulee just over a month. He had been staying at the Packhorse Hotel, waiting for a chance to buy a spread at a reasonable price. He had the money. It was in the bank at Green Coulee – every one of the ten thousand dollars blood money he had earned as a bounty hunter!

There were odd events going on in a town that boasted a system of law and order. When the ranni-gans from outlying ranches rode into town for a spree and started free fights, the inhabitants merely sighed, realising this was the way of the west. It was not the boisterous shooting-play that jagged Jack Griffin's stern sense of law. It was the undercurrent of crooked-ness that held certain leading inhabitants that griped him.

Sheriff Tom Mortimer was getting old. Jack had sensed that Tom was averse to cleaning up. Maybe it was because he was getting old, and maybe it was something else. Jack did not know.

'I'll have to buy me that spread,' muttered Jack as his horse jogged along. 'I'll have to mind my own business. Ain't nothin' to me if Ern Spiceland has got cows thet don't belong to him. Though I never figgered Ern to be a rustler, short time I known him! An' if Sam Brant goes gits himself shot up, is thet my business? Shore figger I'll buy that Box-T spread at the far end o' the plain and buy me a good hoss.'

He could only conclude he was taking on the job of lawman through sheer force of habit. He had spent three years chasing bad-men; he could spend a little more time until he was ready to buy that ranch. There was really little incentive for a man to become a deputy, except the urge to take sides with the law.

It was a good hour later when Jack rode his horse into Green Coulee. The town lay under the afternoon heat, with a few loungers taking it easy in front of the saloons. An occasional buckboard rattled through the dusty main street, and a lone rider, caked with sweat and dust, rode slowly down the middle of the street.

Jack rode quickly up to the sheriff's office. The building was one of the few brick-built places in town. He tied his horse at the rail and walked stiffly on to the boardwalk. His head still ached.

He walked in and went down a passage to the office which served Tom Mortimer as a home from home. He expected to find the rugged old-timer sitting at the desk, staring at the three empty cells across the room.

But Tom was not in the office.

Jack looked around with inquiring eyes. He went over to a bench at the rear of the big room. There was some water in a jug and a dish nearby. He took off his stetson and used some of the water to wash the bruise on his head. A few minutes later he felt more comfortable. The throb-throb had gone. He went into the living-room of the building and looked round for sign of Sam Brant.

'Quiet!' he muttered. 'I thought that hombre could not be moved?'

His steady eyes were puzzled and wary. He had left the deputy sheriff a badly wounded man. Tom Mortimer and Bertram Wast had been attending him. Yet Sam Brant was not in the bed in the living-room of the sheriff's office.

Jack went out to the tie-rail and got his horse. He thought he would go along to the Red Pine saloon. He might find Tom Mortimer there.

Jack rode the horse slowly to the saloon and dismounted. In the afternoon, the street was almost deserted. Three men on the verandah of the Red Pine stared at Jack. They made no comment as he walked to the batwing doors, his high-heel boots making a sharp sound on the boards. One man flicked his eyes over the deputy sheriff badge which Jack still wore on his shirt.

Jack pushed through the doors and stopped. He fumbled in his shirt pocket for the 'makings'. He began to roll the cigarette. He only moved forward as he struck a match to light the smoke. He saw Tom Mortimer sitting at a table with another man.

'Ern got away, Tom,' drawled Jack, and he stared down at the two men.

Sheriff Tom Mortimer looked up at the younger man from under his bushy eyebrows.

'Gott'n away! Hell, Jack I thought I told yuh to bring him to me without any fightin'!'

Jack Griffin smiled.

'Wasn't any fightin' tuh mention. I just got a bump on the head. Ern rode off. Maybe he's back on his spread. I don't know. All I want tuh say is that I've changed my mind about being yore deputy, Tom. I came to Green Coulee tuh settle down – buy me a ranch. I shouldn't ha' ridden out after Ern Spiceland. I don't even know why yuh want him.'

'I told yuh, Jack!' Tom Mortimer bluffed. He looked worriedly at Wast. He stroked his black moustache with gnarled fingers – as if he were anxious about something.

'So yuh couldn't keep a hombre by yore side!' mocked the big man in store clothes, who sat beside Tom.

Jack looked down warily at Bertram Wast. This man was the wealthy owner of the big Bar-K outfit. This was the man who, only five years ago, had arrived at Green Coulee a stranger with money. Now, due to clever manipulations of loans, he owned all the range round the cow town. Not until a man rode more than half a day did he sight the land of other ranchers in the county. Rumours were that Wast had managed most of this prosperity by cunning moves, hardness and duplicity.

'Maybe I was too blamed friendly,' admitted Jack. 'I

11

shore didn't expect Ern tuh hit me on the head. And yuh haven't explained, Tom. Yuh just said Ern had cows on his spread that didn't belong there. Yuh didn't say if those cows had worked-over brands or had just strayed.'

'Strayed nothin'!' snapped Bertram Wast. 'I'll tell you, Griffin. Those longhorns on Spiceland's ranch are Bar-K cattle. Maybe they have worked-over brands. We don't know until we see 'em. And they didn't stray because Spiceland is busy fencing his east boundary. He's got wire and posts strung up.'

'Fencing his water-holes maybe,' drawled Jack. 'Anyway I'm tellin' yuh, Tom, I'm not the deputy sheriff any longer. There's too many things I don't rightly understand, and you ain't explaining.'

Tom Mortimer did not look at Jack. Instead he reached savagely for his drink and gulped it.

'What happened to Sam Brant?' Jack asked quietly. 'I don't figure he got up and walked away.'

'Yore blamed right, he didn't!' growled Tom. 'He's dead. He's buried now.'

Jack blew smoke for a few seconds before replying.

'Mighty quick drop to boothill,' he said. 'He was suffering from lead poisonin', but I didn't figure he'd die.'

'Wal, he did, plumb quick. so we buried him, same as we'd do for anyone else.'

'Reckon that makes Mike Capstaff a murderer,' said Jack quietly. 'Because it wasn't a fair gun play.'

'We'll get him,' growled Tom Mortimer, and he looked anxiously at Bertram Wast.

Jack saw the quick glance and wondered why Tom was so worried about placating the owner of the Bar-K.

Jack Griffin began to unclip the deputy badge from his shirt. Tom Mortimer rose suddenly and put out a detaining hand.

'Wear that badge a mite longer, Jack!' he pleaded. 'I need a deputy.'

'Maybe yuh'll get around to explainin' about Ern Spiceland?' questioned Jack mockingly.

'Maybe I will, son,' said the old-timer hurriedly. 'But jest you keep that badge on yore shirt.'

Jack fastened it slowly. Without another word he walked to the bar. He ordered a drink from the fat bartender. As he stood at the pine counter, he was wondering just how guilty Ern Spiceland was of rustling.

Jack was a tall, lean man. Under the black gaber-dine shirt, iron-hard muscles rippled. One gun lay low on his right thigh, in a dark, shiny holster. He was wearing blue jeans over which were leather, bat-wing chaps. There was nothing fancy or ornamental about his holster belt, but he did wear leather cuffs just above the wrists which were studded with gleaming brass. His grey stetson capped dark, thick hair. His eyes were often startlingly blue up against his sun-reddened face.

The saloon was not very busy, for most of the men were at work on the distant spreads, but a few ranni-gans were propped against the bar. In a corner a gambler in a black suit played a straight-faced game with a rancher who had had more than enough whisky.

Jack turned, figuring it was time he went back to his hotel. The shot of whisky made him feel affable. He waved to old Tom Mortimer as he went past him. Jack did not greet Wast with any friendliness. There was something about the man he did not like. Maybe it was the rumours he had heard in the few weeks he had been back in town. Maybe he was prejudiced. But he did not like Wast.

Jack rode his horse along to the livery. He paid the stable-jack and walked out. His own custom-built saddle was with his luggage at the hotel. He strolled along to the Packhorse Hotel and then halted and turned inquiring eyes into the sun as he heard shots ring out.

Shooting did not bring many people to their feet in Green Coulee. But Jack went back, sensing the position of the shots.

He started back to the Red Pine saloon with long strides. Just as he sighted the saloon, a man hurtled out and jumped to his horse. Even as he rowelled the horse cruelly, he snapped two more shots at the batwing doors. The rider was almost out of the town before two men spilled from the bar and climbed on horses to set off in chase. By then Jack was at the batwing doors. He was not sure what he would find. But a queer tickling feeling in the nape of his neck made him grimly expectant.

The shots could be two waddies making free with some lead just for the fun or because they were trigger happy. But maybe it was something else. As deputy sheriff, it was his business.

He went through the doors of the saloon with wary eyes alert for lightning reaction. His hand was near his Colt. It did strike him that if he were to continue as

14

deputy sheriff, he would have to buckle on another holster belt and fill it with a hogleg.

On the floor of the saloon lay the body of a man, and around it clustered half a dozen men. As Jack strode forward, he saw Bertram Wast. The big man was by the side of the body. Jack went forward and looked over Wast's shoulder.

Jack stared into the contorted face of Tom Mortimer. A .48 slug had shattered a hole in the sheriff's heart. Blood swelled sullenly round his shirt and vest.

'Who did it?' asked Jack Griffin harshly.

Bertram Wast rose to his feet. He dusted his hands as if there were nothing more final than death.

'It was Mike Capstaff,' he said briefly.

'That hombre again!' exclaimed Jack, and he looked at the others interrogatively.

'He came in like a galoot that's plumb lookin' for gun-play!' rasped the fat bartender.

'Shore was!' drawled another cowpuncher. 'Sheriff went for his smoke-pole, but that ranny was too fast.'

'Why should that owl-hoot kill old Tom?' rapped Jack.

'Seems like Tom Mortimer and Sam Brant got on the wrong side o' Mike Capstaff,' drawled Bertram Wast.

Jack Griffin was caustic.

'Couldn't one o' you hombres put a slug in that outlaw's belly?'

'He sure made a fast play,' said the bartender, aggrieved. 'That jigger was in and out in a matter o' seconds. I guess he had a hoss waitin'.'

15

'I don't suppose he had a railroad ticket!' said Jack sarcastically. 'Hope those two fellers after him hit him with lead!'

Bertram Wast picked up his unfinished drink from the table at which he had so recently sat with the sheriff. He drank it off with a gesture. He smacked his lips.

'Wal, I guess this town needs a new sheriff,' he said casually.

He made for the batwing doors, a big man in black store suit. Jack wondered for a second if he packed a gun. There was no sign of one, but the rancher could carry a hidden Derringer. He looked the type.

'Wait!'

Jack snapped out the word. Wast stopped at the batwings. His dark strong face inquiring.

'In case you forget,' drawled Jack. 'I'm the deputy sheriff in the meantime. An' I'm sending a posse after that outlaw! Maybe we kin catch up with him. But he's got a head start, an' he got away once before jest like this.'

'I figured you were turning the job in,' said Wast smoothly.

Jack touched the badge on his shirt. He looked down at Tom Mortimer. When his eyes flicked the others in the saloon again, his face was grim. Jack turned, looked at the few citizens crowding round the batwing doors.

'Tom was a good feller,' he said. 'Maybe he made mistakes. Maybe he was gettin' old. He sure seemed to me like a hombre with troubles on his mind. Anyway, he swore me in as deputy, and I'll keep the job in the meantime. In fact, if yuh want a full-time sheriff, I'll stand for the job – until I git me a ranch.'

'Judge Tarrant, over in Abilene, is the gent who'll decide on a new sheriff for Green Coulee,' drawled Bertram Wast.

'Shore. I'll abide by the judge's decision,' said Jack.

He went towards the batwing doors. Doc Turner, who was also the town's undertaker, was looking at the dead sheriff and muttering under his breath.

'Nuthin' but shootin's! If I patch 'em up, they got to pay me. If I put 'em in a casket, the town funds got to pay. Figure I can't lose anyway!'

Grimly, Jack went among the punchers outside and got three men to agree to ride after the other two who had chased Mike Capstaff. The men climbed to horses immediately, and Jack gave them a last word.

'I figger that owl-hoot disappears as soon as he hits them hills. But yuh kin try to find his sign. Reckon I'll stick here an' look into Tom Mortimer's desk. Might pick up a clue.'

But there was a big query. Why had Mike Capstaff come into town and shot Sam Brant and Tom Mortimer? At first, the shooting of Sam Brant had seemed like an accidental clash. But the outlaw had returned and murdered the sheriff. There was a deliberate intention behind it all.

Jack went to the Packhorse Hotel. He went up to the second floor, where he had rented a room. Inside his room, he opened a saddle pack. He brought out a holster belt and slowly strapped it round his waist. He adjusted it until the shiny holster hung low on his left thigh. Then he got another Colt out of the pack. He examined it, saw that it was loaded and working easily. He slipped it into the empty holster.

'Two guns are better than one,' he muttered.

He made his way to the street and walked along to the sheriff's office. Now that there was no actual sheriff, he was in charge. He began to look through the few documents that Tom Mortimer had kept.

But he found nothing which would throw light on Tom Mortimer's intention to question Ern Spiceland about rustled cattle on his spread. Apparently Tom Mortimer kept his records in his head – and he was dead now.

Jack leafed through some old descriptions of wanted men. There was nothing of interest. Nothing on Mike Capstaff, so there was no connection here, either.

He went out to the street again and made his way to the livery.

There was one thing he needed, and that was a good horse which he could call his own. When he had landed in Green Coulee a few weeks ago he had come in on the stage which ran from the railroad station at Abilene some twenty miles away. And from then on, he had hired a horse for the little amount of riding he had done.

Jack Griffin went into the livery and found the proprietor. A few words, and he was led to the stall where he had last seen the big roan. It was a good horse, tall and proud. Jack had noticed it earlier.

'Want to sell?' he asked the liveryman.

'Shore. Make me an offer.'

And Jack made an offer.

Five minutes later he walked quickly out of the Packhorse Hotel with his custom-built saddle, bed-roll, lariat and rifle. He rigged the horse quickly, pushed the rifle into the saddle holster and rode out of the livery.

The roan was good. The horse had spirit and pride. It had been well treated. Jack figured the roan would suit him. There was speed in those trim legs, too.

Jack Griffin was riding slowly along to the sheriff's office with the intention of hitching the roan to the tie-rail while he settled in. He saw the stage rattle in with a pounding of hoofs and a cloud of dust. It was the daily stage from Abilene.

As he rode alongside, curious like the rest of the townspeople, he saw a girl alight. She was about the third passenger off, and a young fellow assisted her to the dusty street.

The girl was dressed in a long coat which had a swing from the waist. Under the hat, corn-coloured hair rioted in a mass of curls. Her face was set and rather stern, yet this did not detract from the charm and clean-cut loveliness of her features.

The young man who helped the girl down from the high steps of the stage instantly reminded Jack Griffin of Ern Spiceland.

The resemblance was so remarkable that Jack jigged his roan nearer, his eyes crinkled at the corners with wariness.

The young man was something of a dandy, in a light suit which had obviously been made in an eastern city. He wore a dark hat and a black tie.

Jack Griffin dismounted, threw the reins over a

19

nearby tie-rail, and walked closer to the girl and young fellow. For a few seconds, as the luggage was being got out of the stage, he studied the youngster. Then he came closer.

'I'm the deputy sheriff,' he said with a smile. 'Name o' Jack Griffin.'

The young man turned. He had the same bright eyes as Ern Spiceland. Jack plunged on.

'Care to tell me yore name, stranger?'

The young man in the dandy suit gave a ready smile.

'Certainly, Mr Griffin. In fact, you're just the man we want to see. I'm Fred Spiceland, and this is my sister Jane. We're Ern's brother and sister. Just this morning we heard Ern was in trouble, and we've come right over to see him. We hear Ern tangled with the sheriff. Is that right, Mr Griffin?'

Jack nodded, glancing briefly at the girl,.

'It's right to a certain extent, but Sheriff Mortimer is dead now, and I intend to investigate the whole durned business.'

'I can't believe Ern would rustle cattle,' said Jane Spiceland clearly.

'How did you hear all this?' Jack smiled.

'A friend came on the morning stage to Abilene,' Fred explained. 'Seems the news kinda circulated around the saloons soon as you rode out. What happened, Deputy? Where is Ern? How come Sheriff Mortimer is dead?'

'An owl-hoot by the name o' Mike Capstaff killed Mortimer,' said Jack briefly. 'Sam Brant, the deputy before me, was shot by the same hombre. I went out to

20

get Ern and bring him back to town for questionin', but he tricked me. I don't know where he is. But I kin promise yuh Ern will get a fair hearin' as long as I'm deputy. Seein' yore Ern's brother and sister, I can tell yuh I'm not satisfied about the allegations concerning Ern – and I'm plumb mad about the killin' of Tom Mortimer and Sam Brant. I aim tuh find out why they were killed.'

'Just as soon as we change, we're ridin' out to Ern's ranch,' said Jane Spiceland determinedly.

They parted. Jack stared reflectively as they went to the Packhorse Hotel.

2
Battle at Round-O

Jack Griffin was waiting outside the Packhorse Hotel some fifteen minutes later. He was waiting to see Jane Spiceland and her brother. He had the roan all ready for an afternoon's' ride. He thought he would ride out with Jane and Fred and try to get to the bottom of the rustling allegation against Ern.

While he was waiting, two men rode into the dusty street. One clutched a wound in his shoulder. Jack recognised the men as the hombres who had chased after Capstaff.

'Bad luck,' said one man. 'My hoss went lame, an' Bud here stopped some lead. Had tuh turn back. I saw the other three fellers ridin' out, but they'll never catch Mike Capstaff. He'll hit the hills afore them.'

Jack nodded grimly. Getting the outlaw would be a long-term job now, he felt.

He was agreeably surprised when Jane came out and went round to the hotel livery. He left his horse and walked over. She had changed from her city clothes to range garb. She looked like a slim youth in blue jeans tucked into riding boots. She wore a red shirt and yellow bandanna, which matched the riot of golden hair which peeped out from under her fawn stetson.

'I'll ride over with yuh,' said Jack briefly.

Fred was still wearing his city suit, but he had donned high-heel cowboy boots, and his trousers were tucked into them.

'I want to see Ern,' said Jack, 'if he's still around.'

'Why shouldn't Ern be around?' asked the girl.

'Wal, I'm the law, an' he hit me mighty hard with his big fist,' drawled Jack Griffin. 'And, Miss, to be quite candid, he left me kinda helpless out in the Panhandle. But maybe I'll forget that if he can do some explainin'. I want tuh know why he was afraid to come to town.'

'There are plenty of things we want to know,' added Jane, determinedly.

'Ern always was a queer cuss,' said Fred. 'I'm the youngest, you know. D'you figure I look more than nineteen, Mister Griffin?'

Jack smiled.

'Maybe. I think yuh need some range ridin'. What do yuh work at back in Abilene?'

'I'm studying to be a lawyer,' said Fred eagerly. 'Plenty of scope in the West for a good lawyer! Jane teaches the kids in the school at Abilene. Mighty good teacher, is Jane.'

23

His eager words brought a flush to the girl's cheeks, and she turned away to talk to the liveryman about a horse.

Some ten minutes later all three rode out of Green Coulee. The sun was high and brassy. Heat shimmers distorted the horizon. The flat Panhandle stretched for miles, and in the far distance were the dull blurs of the rising foothills. This broken ground was the location of Ern's Round-O Ranch. It was poor land for cattle. The hardy longhorns had to move constantly to find fresh grass among the mesquite and catsclaw. They had to travel so much, they were pretty lean creatures.

The foothills marked the western end of the Panhandle plain. The broken ground, studded with rocky spurs and buttes, rose slowly, mile after mile, into small canyons and hilly ridges. Only cholla cactus and Joshua trees grew here, although the floors of the canyons were a veritable forest of catsclaw and mesquite bush. It was late in the afternoon when they rode slowly closer and closer to Ern Spiceland's ranch. The ranch-house and pole corrals became visible through the heat shimmers. They passed some steers that jumped nervously at the approach of horses. Jack got a view of the Round-O brand worked into their hides. So far as he could see, there were no worked-over brands. But, naturally, if he wanted to find some cattle bearing brands altered from Bar-K to Round-O he would have to look hard for them.

The way he figured it, Ern would be crazy to try to alter the brands, anyhow. They certainly would not alter easily.

24

Jack Griffin was ahead of Jane and Fred Spiceland when he heard the sudden sound of shots. His instinctive reaction was to rowel the roan gently with his spurs. The horse sprang forward. There was a defined trail leading to the ranch. The roan flew along. Jack had ridden that way earlier that day. Soon all the details of the ranch were clear to his eyes. The buildings lay in a slight hollow. There were no cottonwoods to give shade, as in the case of so many spreads. But Jack could see figures of men, and they were hiding behind the barn. He heard the snap of Colt-fire, and then the bark of a rifle. He saw the lurking men fire at the ranch-house.

Jack Griffin realised he was the only one with guns. Fred and Jane were not armed. Fred, it seemed, was more at home with a pen and law books. Jane, for all her determination, was only a girl.

Jack eased out his .48 Colt. With a thunder of hoofs, the roan tore up to the ranch. The horse cleared a pole fence and came up behind the barn. Jack began to fire as soon as the roan steadied after the jump.

He knew the difficulties of aiming with a short-barrelled gun from a moving horse, but he also knew he had killed more than one bad man that way.

He had seen the answering fire from the ranch-house, and he had figured out the situation. Ern Spiceland was in the ranch-house, and these hombres firing at him had no right to be doing just that.

The roan reared as he fired.

Crack! Crack!

The two men had wheeled at his approach. They crouched and fired. They each held a gun in each hand. They had the advantage of being steady on their feet. But it was only a momentary advantage.

Jack sat the saddle and had his hardware out from both holsters. He snapped fast shots at the two men. His roan pranced with fright. A slug tore at his hat. The movement of the horse made him a difficult target, even if it added to his trouble in aiming. Shots roared in all directions. One of the men pitched forward like a dummy. The other, darting a desperate glance to right and left, leaped backwards around the barn.

Jack reloaded one Colt quickly, even as he jigged his horse after the man. The reins were slack around the horse's neck. The animal responded intelligently to the pressure of Jack's knees.

The roan jigged round the barn, and Jack took a shot at the escaping man. He saw the man clutch his arm and howl. Then the fellow darted round a big stack of logs.

Jack heard the sound of hoofs and knew the man had a horse hidden behind the log-pile. He was about to go after him when something else claimed his attention.

Apparently there were three men, for, all at once, another man rode round the ranch-house. His horse was dragging a chain to which was attached a big bundle of blazing tree branches. Swiftly as an Indian, the man rode up to the gable end of the ranch. There were no windows, and Ern Spiceland could not see him. The man whipped the burning brushwood against the ranch-house wall. Even as Jack rowelled his horse forward, the man threw off the drag chain and spurred his horse cruelly.

Jack Griffin emptied his Colt after the escaping man. But the rider had the devil's own luck. He seemed to be unhit.

Jack had to stop. He leaped from the roan and ran up to the blazing wood. He began to kick it away. Already the wood had charred deeply into the side of the ranch-house. It seemed as though the burning wood had been dipped in some inflammable substance. The whole exploit had been planned, evidently.

For some few minutes Jack Griffin was involved in frantic kicking and stamping at the burning bale of wood. He got the main part clear and he kicked at the charred side of the building. Soon the fire was under control, and at that moment he was aware he had been joined by the others. He looked and saw Ern Spiceland's bright eyes and swarthy face beside him.

'Those galoots want tuh burn yuh out, Ern!' drawled Jack.

'Yeah. And they kinda want tuh kill me, too,' supplied Ern. 'They're Bar-K men.'

'Bertram Wast's hands!' exclaimed Jack. 'You shore?'

'Come round here and see the hombre yuh plugged,' grunted Ern.

He walked away, a tall, lean figure in flapping chaps and vest. Jack went forward, dusting the burnt charcoal from his hands. Fred and Jane moved after their brother. So far, there had not been much time for greetings and explanations.

The dead man was an unshaven individual in dirty range clothes. Jack's bullet had hit him between the eyes, drilling a neat hole.

27

'In spite o' the slug spoilin' his face, I recognise this hombre,' said Ern. 'He is Jed Slacks. Works for Wast.'

'Can't say I know him,' muttered Jack. 'But that's nothin', seeing I've bin here only a few weeks. Look, Ern, what's goin' on? How come I find these galoots tryin' tuh burn yuh out?'

'I don't know,' rasped Ern. 'I tell yuh, I jest don't know. But I know who's tryin' tuh get me out o' this ranch.'

'Who?'

'Bertram Wast.'

'But he's got the biggest ranch in this part o' the Panhandle,' argued Jack. 'Why should that feller try to git yuh out o' the Round-O?'

'I've jest told yuh – I don't know!'

Ern Spiceland looked at his brother and sister and grinned, as if he had ignored them long enough.

'Howdy, Fred! Why, Jane, you shore look prettier than ever! How come yuh ridin' out here with the deputy sheriff?'

'We heard about you tangling with Tom Mortimer,' exclaimed the girl. 'We came over from Abilene, not knowing what to expect.'

'Sure, Ern. Guess we haven't seen you for a long time,' put in Fred.

'Nope. Well, yuh're seeing me now. Tom Mortimer isn't gettin' me in his lock-up.' Ern Spiceland swung to Jack. 'I've figured it out. Wast is tryin' to pin something on me. I ain't put an iron to one o' his steers. My longhorns are my own, Griffin. Maybe I should have told yuh this instead o' flinging my fists at yuh! But I figured yuh were workin' for Tom Mortimer and Wast.

I fought yuh after I had figured I was crazy to ride into town for Wast to frame me.'

'You can count Tom Mortimer out now,' said Jack quietly.

'Can I? How come? That old buzzard has shore got himself under Bertram Wast's little finger.'

'He's dead, Ern. Mike Capstaff walked into the Red Pine and shot old Tom. Can yuh give me any ideas on that, Ern?

Ern Spiceland scanned the bronzed face of the man before him as if the words were difficult to assimilate. Then Ern's bright eyes hardened.

'Maybe I got no real ideas, but I got a hunch. Wast had Tom Mortimer just like that!' Ern made a gesture with his fingers. 'I can't prove nuthin'. But I've got the hunch that says I'm right. Figger it out for yoreself, Griffin. Mike Capstaff didn't shoot Tom Mortimer for nuthin'. and it weren't no accident Sam Brant got shot like yuh told me. No, sir. It ain't no accident – that's all I kin say!'

'Sam Brant is more'n shot, Ern. He's dead.'

Ern Spiceland did not say anything. He just stared at Jack and then slowly took from his vest pocket the 'makings'. He rolled the cigarette expertly and shook his head as if depressed by the news of Sam Brant's death.

'Dead!' he repeated. 'I'm right. Somethin' queer's goin' on!'

They walked round to the front of the ranch. The house was mill-cut timber, for there was no standing timber for miles around. It was a modest little ranch-house of three rooms, with a stone-built chimney

29

rising from the ground level on one gable end. As they went on to the verandah, Ern turned and scanned the horizon.

'That bandy rannigan who works for me ought tuh be back from Green Coulee,' he muttered. 'Anyways, set yoreselves in and I'll get some chow. Guess yuh could do with some coffee, Jane?'

But the girl was near the stove already.

'I may be a school-marm, but I can cook,' she laughed. 'And, if I remember rightly, your coffee is so black it chokes me.'

While the three were talking and getting ready to drink and eat, Jack Griffin went out to the verandah again. He was sorely puzzled. He was beginning to realise there was a deep play going on. If the dead man had been in Bertram Wast's employ, there was some explaining to be done by the owner of the Bar-K. Of course, Wast would disclaim any responsibility, but that would not obviate the need for inquiries to be made. And as deputy sheriff the task would fall to him. Already he was up against Bertram Wast. But why should the Bar-K owner, with his vast spread, desire to force Ern Spiceland off his poor ranch?

While Jack pondered the problems, he noticed a cloud of dust on the horizon. Slowly it came nearer, until he could distinguish the buckboard and horses responsible for the dust. The outfit came on at a good lick, and finally rattled into the ranch yard. A thick-set little man came rolling up to Jack.

'Howdy, Deputy!' hailed the broad little man. 'I'm Bandy Manners. Work for Ern. I'm a goldarned cook, swamper and cowpuncher rolled into one. Yuh here to arrest Ern again?'

'I ain't arrestin' anyone – yet,' said Jack.

'Yuh got sense,' said the little man shrewdly.

As they turned to go inside the ranch-house, Jack said: 'I figure I might want that buckboard to take a dead man tuh Green Coulee. I don't like ridin' with dead men on my hoss.'

'Dead man! Say, who's dead now?'

Jack Griffin told him, and jerked a hand to indicate the side of the ranch-house where they had left the body.

'Bar-K hombre, huh?' grunted Bandy Manners. 'That's bad. Wast won't like that.'

'You know any good reason why Wast should make a play tuh git Ern out o' this ranch?'

'Nary an idee!'

'D'you figure Wast wants this spread for some reason?'

'I figger Wast is tryin' tuh run Ern off this range. That hombre wouldn't let a jack-rabbit live. I've seen Bar-K riders up in the foothills. Ern has filed claim on all that land.'

'What were the riders doin'?'

'Nuthin', so far as I could see. Just ridin' around. I couldn't figure out why.'

Jack Griffin had to 'set to' with the others and enjoy the rough hospitality offered by Ern Spiceland with the assistance of Jane. There was plenty of beans, bacon and coffee.

'Thanks for the grub,' said Jack wryly. 'In exchange, I'll forget about that bang on the head.'

But there was work to do.

'I'm deputy sheriff, Ern,' he said slowly, 'and I want a look round yore beef. Wast makes allegations, Ern, and so I just got to look into them. I figure we could ride around and git a good look at your stock.'

'Yuh're wasting your time,' stated Ern, 'but I'll be glad to show yuh around. If there's any Bar-K cattle on my range, they're strays.'

'I'm lookin' for worked-over brands,' said Jack.

'Yuh won't find any.'

Bandy Manners was bristling, but he subsided after a little thought on his part. He realised that Jack, as deputy sheriff, had to be impartial.

They set off a little later, leaving the ranch in charge of Bandy Manners. Jane would not be deterred from going with the three men, although Ern warned her they would have to complete a good hour of hard riding.

There was just time to ride around part of the ranch and look at some stock and then get back to Green Coulee before the sun dipped in a red blaze on the west.

They found some longhorns on the plain. The four riders hazed the cattle into a group, and then Jack went around examining the brands. It was necessarily swift work. He found the steers were all clearly Round-O stock. They rode away into the rising buttes of the broken, semi-arid land. Ern had said there were some small herds in the canyons. Many cows were following a lead steer. Ern was quite willing to show Jack Griffin as much stock as possible in the limited time.

They rode into the mesquite-covered floor of a small canyon. A bunch of cows were nosing through a patch of mesquite grass at the far end. The lean long-horns lifted heads as the riders approached, but they could not get out of the canyon, although they tried to lumber away at the approach of the intruders.

Jack Griffin's attitude was merely that of a man doing his duty. Bertram Wast had made accusations, and so the matter must be settled. The job had been Tom Mortimer's until his death, although now it was not quite clear just how much Tom had believed in the allegations.

The beef was hazed into a bunch by Ern and Fred, and Jack went among the bawling cattle to examine the brands. It was merely a question of a quick glance, but he did not intend to miss one animal. If he was satisfied in his own mind he could reply to Bertram Wast with confidence.

And then, suddenly, he saw the Bar-K brand with a worked-over Round-O. The superimposed brand was badly done. Usually, in a case of rustling where altered brands were concerned, cattle with old brands were selected. The old brand was then roughed out alto-gether and a new brand burned deeply. But with this Texas longhorn, the Round-O brand had been clum-sily burnt over the old Bar-K marks, making the whole thing obvious to anyone at first sight.

With a grave face, Jack pointed at the animal. The others saw his gesture. Ern's face darkened grimly.

There were other longhorns in the herd similarly worked-over. Jack counted twelve cows in the small herd that had followed a lead steer into the canyon, and those twelve cows bore clumsily altered brands.

Jack rode out of the herd, gestured to Ern to follow,

and rode down the canyon a little way out of the bawling of the disturbed cattle. Fred and Jane followed in
silence, wondering.

Jack Griffin leaned forward with his hands on the
saddle horn.

'How d'you figure that beef got there?' he asked
quietly.

Ern Spiceland was angry.

'Listen here, Jack, yuh kin see with yore own eyes
that this set-up is a fake! Do you figure I'd bring yuh
along to see stolen cattle? Do yuh think I knew about
those longhorns?'

'Are they yore cattle, Ern?'

'No, by Gawd! Now ask me who altered those
brands!'

'I sure will. Who altered them, Ern?'

'Not me, I kin tell yuh! But I kin guess. Wast had
those cattle worked-over and then herded on to my
range. He's tryin' to pin something on me. He wants
me off'n this land for some reason!'

'You say they are not yore cows,' commented Jack.
'Yuh didn't buy them? Yuh haven' a bill o' sale?'

'I got no bill o' sale, and I didn't buy them off'n
Wast,' said Ern Spiceland violently.

Jack gave a tight-lipped grin.

'Keep yore hair on, Ern! I'm only askin' questions.
The way I see it, yuh're framed pretty nicely. Wast has
only to lead a posse of men from Green Coulee to look
over these beefs, and yuh know the general conclusion
would be that yuh rustled them. The cattlemen round
here don't like rustlers. There was a bit of that in the
past, an' they've just stamped it out, so I hear.'

Ern shifted grimly in his saddle and flashed a glance at his brother and sister. They were quiet, realising this serious situation needed sorting out.

'How come yuh don't believe I've stolen this beef?' jerked Ern.

'Because only a blamed fool would leave them in this canyon so near to yore ranch. An' if you'd known the beef was here, yuh wouldn't have brought me along to find 'em. I can see the circumstances that are against yuh, Ern. And I can also see the facts that are in yore favour. But if Wast wants to work up somethin', he can sure make it stick. I wonder how long these longhorns have been here?'

Ern moved his head quickly, glanced at the wide sweep of the mesquite-covered canyon.

'Day or two, most likely, by the look o' the grass – or what's left o' it. I ain't been here myself for more'n a week.'

Jack raised his head and looked at the dying sun.

'Let's get goin'. Nothin' yuh can do about these longhorns tonight.'

'What the heck can I do about them in any case?'

'Yuh can do plenty when we find the hombres who did the work of branding,' said Jack swiftly.

Ern slapped a fist into the palm of his other hand.

'Shore! That would prove the whole thing a blamed fake.'

'It won't be easy,' warned Jack. 'But as long as I'm deputy, I'm not making an arrest on these circumstances. An' I aim tuh find out who were the rannigans who actually did the job. If yuh can get one o' them to spill the beans, the frame-up falls to pieces.'

They turned their horse's heads and rode slowly out of the canyon. They were deep in thought. Finally they reached the Round-O ranch yard, and Bandy Manners came out to greet them. He had the dead man loaded on to the buckboard.

'Yuh want me to drive this dead 'un into town?' he yelled at Jack Griffin.

'Nope,' Jack answered back with a grin that crinkled the corners of his wary eyes. 'I'll take the loan of the buckboard an' drive this galoot back to town myself. I want some citizens to identify him as Wast's hired hand. My horse can follow on a lead. You an' Ern got a job to do.'

'What's that?' Ern turned to Jack.

'Get those longhorns outa that canyon. Get them hidden somewheres in the hills. Remember, I'm the deputy sheriff, an' I didn't tell yuh this. It's unofficial. But git them cattle away so that Wast can't prove anythin' if he decides he wants to. In the meantime, I reckon to find the gents that did the branding job. It's pretty certain Wast didn't heat the irons himself.'

'Yuh give me durned good advice,' muttered Ern.

Bandy Manners did not understand, and he had to be told about the cattle in the canyon. The little man's whiskers bristled in anger.

'Why, durn it, there's only me and Ern on this spread, and yuh can take it from me we didn't put no iron tuh Bar-K cattle!'

'Right,' said Jack with a tight smile. 'Yuh know what to do. Must be some place where those beefs can be hidden. It's yore only defence, Ern, against a sudden move by Wast. Because he knows the worked-over

36

cattle are on yore spread. But if yuh hide them and he can't produce them as evidence, yuh've beaten him. Wal, I've got to take this stiff back for burial.'

Jack hitched the roan to the back of the buckboard and then climbed on board.

'We're staying in Green Coulee for a day or two,' Jane called to her brother. 'We'll ride over tomorrow. There must be something we can do to help.'

'Sorry, I can't put you up tonight,' Ern exclaimed. 'But we've only got two bunks, and even if Bandy and I slept somewheres else, the bunks are not good enough for you, Jane . . . Don't rightly know about yuh though, Fred! Want to stay the night?'

'I reckon I'd better go along with Jane.'

'Yeah, reckon that's best. Take care o' her, Fred.'

Jack jerked at the traces, and the buckboard rattled out of the dusty ranch yard. Jane and Fred followed on their hired horses. The little party soon left the Round-O buildings and travelled swiftly towards the distant Green Coulee.

When they entered the town, lights from kerosene lamps were sending straggling beams into the main street. Jane and Fred said adios to Jack and went into their hotel, tired and hungry after a long day.

Jack Griffin had sterner duties. He left the buckboard outside the sheriff's office and carried the dead man inside. He went along for Doc Turner. The old medico man lived in a pretentious clapboard house at the end of the town. When Jack found him, he was drinking whisky in his surgery. He was not too pleased at being asked to go out and examine a dead man.

'Dead, huh? Can't he wait until morn? Never heard of a dead man that couldn't wait!'

'I want him certified dead, identified, and buried,' said Jack grimly.

Doc Turner peered at him over his steel-rimmed spectacles.

'You ought to be sheriff, young man. All right, let's go.'

On the way back, Jack stopped at a closed store. He knocked and soon collected another citizen. This was Al Bride, a storekeeper who knew everyone in town and on the outlying spreads for miles around.

'I want you to identify a dead hombre,' Jack told him. 'An' I want you to certify him dead, Doc. It's all for the records. Once I've got them, I can hand the body over to the grave-digger on Boot Hill. I've moved into the sheriff's office, and I sure don't like bodies lyin' around!'

They tramped along the boardwalks and presently reached the brick wall of the sheriff's office. Jack had left the door open, following the free and easy custom of the days. They walked in, along the passage that flanked the living quarters, and then into the office.

Jack Griffin halted abruptly. He had left a dead man lying on the floor.

Right now, the office was empty. He had a sudden feeling of unreality. There was no body on the floor.

He went swiftly to the cells, wondering if someone had entered during his absence and played a joke. But the cells were empty. He wheeled and stared at the pursed faces of Doc Turner and Al Bride.

'The body has gone. Someone's taken it.'

'Sure it couldn't ha' walked away?' queried Al Bride, and a broad smile cracked the displeasure on his face.

'I tell you the hombre was dead! Somebody came in here an' took it away.'

'Looky, Griffin,' rumbled Doc Turner, 'I'm getting to be an old man, an' I don't like these chilly nights – not after the heat o' the day. So good-night, sir. Find me that body tomorrow. Unless he's walked up Boot Hill!'

Doc Turner and the storekeeper went away feeling that the matter was unimportant. But Jack knew there was some significance in the move. Someone had taken the dead man away, and the reason was because someone did not want the dead hombre identified.

He had a good idea who was responsible for the move.

3

Bushwhackers Sometimes Die

Jack Griffin stood in the sheriff's office and thought it over for a moment. Night was falling, and it seemed that he was momentarily stumped. Of course, Ern Spiceland had identified the dead man as Jed Slacks, but Jack was keen to get a prominent citizen of Green Coulee to testify to the man's identity. Had the body been in the office for Al Bride to examine, even Wast could not have disputed the matter.

It seemed as though the entry of the buckboard into town had been noticed. Wast, or his hands, had worked quickly. Jed Slacks would be taken out into the arid lands, placed in a hole, and covered up.

'All right,' growled Jack. 'So I can't tackle Wast about the hired hand's attempt to burn Ern's ranch-house. But I can work on locatin' the galoots who rebranded those cows. If Ern gets those cows nicely hidden, he's sure spoilt Wast's play.'

There was also the question of getting on Mike Capstaff's trail. And there was more to it than merely grabbing the outlaw and stringing him up for his crimes. He was duty bound to learn just why Tom Mortimer and Sam Brant had been murdered. It seemed obvious now that the outlaw had sought the two men and deliberately murdered them. The reason why had to be found and recorded.

Jack Griffin led the buckboard into an alley beside the office and then unhitched the horse. With his own roan, he led the animals along to the livery near the hotel. The horses would be looked after for the night.

He went back to the sheriff's office. He walked into the living quarters that had been Tom Mortimer's. There was just a living-room with a bunk. Beyond that was a stove in a built-on recess. The quarters were clean and just as good as the room he had vacated in the Packhorse.

He dumped his saddle and bedroll in a corner. He examined his guns and filled them with shells. He took off his hat and felt the bump on his head. The soreness was still there. He thought he should have got old Doc Turner to look at it.

Jack Griffin had an iron constitution which had taken him along many dangerous trails, but he had never considered a man could dispense with sleep. The way he reckoned it, there could easily be a few moves tomorrow, and in the meantime a bit of shuteye was quite in order.

But he locked the doors of the place. He used his own bedroll and got into the bunk after turning down the lamp. His gun-belts hung inches from his head.

41

Unconcernedly, he hummed a little range song as he lay in the bunk. He was thinking his plans to buy the Box-T were going slightly astray. He was the hombre who was tired of chasing bad men, and yet here he was with the office of deputy sheriff and a bad tangle with the leading cattlemen of the district. His plans for a quiet life as a rancher were not materialising.

He fell asleep, thinking that when he finally bought his own spread and packed in the deputy job, it would be a fine thing for a man if he had a wife like, say, Jane Spiceland!

Next day, the early part of the morning was uneventful, except for a short talk with Jane, during which he told her how the body of Jed Slacks had disappeared last night. She was riding over with Fred to see her brother at the Round-O.

'I'll tell Ern what happened,' she promised.

Jack Griffin was standing on the boardwalk outside the office an hour later when Bertram Wast rode up with two of his hands. One man was Otto Tribe, ramrod of the Bar-K. He was a lean, dark-eyed man with a knife scar fully six inches long down the side of his right cheek. He was more than a hard-driving ranch foreman; he was also a swift gunman, and wore two Colts slung low in a fancy one-piece gun-belt. The other man was a hefty-looking fellow of indeterminate age. Jack knew he was completely bald under the floppy sombrero he wore. But he made up for this with a big moustache which was startlingly red. So he was known as Red Holbin, and had never been known as anything else since his arrival in town a year ago.

42

Jack knew the men. In a tough land, they were pretty hard customers.

Jack wheeled, stood with feet squarely apart, and surveyed the men who sat their mounts and looked down at him.

'Mornin', Griffin!' called Bertram Wast.

The Bar-K owner did not look like a rancher. He wore his black suit and hat; only his boots were the usual gear of a cattleman. His pants were folded into the long, high-heel boots. He carried no gun, as far as Jack could see.

'Mornin', Wast!' Jack returned.

Otto Tribe and Red Holbin sat in silence, leaning forward on their saddle horns, surveying him.

'You heard the news?' asked Wast. 'Judge Tarrant is coming over from Abilene by the afternoon stage, and he's bringing a sheriff with him. A hombre by the name o' Trick Grant.'

'Never heard of him,' said Jack calmly. 'Wal, Judge Tarrant can appoint this hombre sheriff, or he can hold an election and let the folks o' this town decide who they want as sheriff.'

'Figure the folks don't care much so long as there's a peace,' returned Wast. 'I've heard this jigger Trick Grant is a smart man. Held a sheriff's job out in Arizona. Thought yuh'd like to know, Griffin. You figure to stay on as deputy?'

'Maybe,' said Jack. 'An' maybe I'll git the folks of Green Coulee to vote for a sheriff. I'll be a candidate, an' if they vote for me they'll know what they're gettin'.'

'D'you figure that to be a smart move, Griffin?

Thought I heard you were lookin' around to set your-self up on your own spread?'

'Plenty o' time,' drawled Jack.

Bertram Wast nodded slowly.

'Guess it's a question of holdin' a conference with Judge Tarrant when he arrives this afternoon.'

'Yuh seem to be mighty interested in the choice of sheriff, Wast!'

Jack caught a glimpse of a flash of expression in Bertram Wast's eyes, and then it was gone. The man had a poker-face again.

'Naturally, I'm interested. As the leading citizen of this town, I know there can't be progress and trade without law and order. I'm interested in law and order, Griffin.'

Jack decided on a bold verbal onslaught.

'Then yuh might be interested to learn that three o' yore hands tried to shoot Ern Spiceland off his ranch yesterday afternoon. I had to plug one. Name o' Jed Slacks. He's dead. But some jigger took the body right out o' this office last night. Now I figger that's not law an' order, Mr Wast.'

Jack saw Otto Tribe and Red Holbin stiffen up in their saddles. Both men shot oblique glances out of narrowed eyes at Bertram Wast.

'Jed Slacks doesn't work for me, Griffin. I fired him two days ago. Sure interested to hear about him, though. I figured he was bad. Seems like he might have been on the raid. Can't figure any other reason why he should be shootin' around the Round-O place.'

Jack saw it was useless to expect the rancher to

44

reveal any useful clues that could be used against him. With a thin smile on his lips, Jack began to busy himself with making a cigarette.

Bertram Wast and his men jigged their horses around. The big rancher called out:

'Adios, Deputy! Just thought you might be interested to hear about Judge Tarrant.'

And then the men rode away, their sleek horses headed for the Red Pine Saloon further down the street. There were private rooms at the back of the Red Pine where a man like Bertram Wast could enjoy the company of his equals.

Jack spent some time in another saloon where some waddies from an outlying spread were making free with the liquor. He asked questions – mainly about Mike Capstaff. He was hoping some waddy had encountered the outlaw out in the Panhandle trails, or maybe some cowboy had cut the man's sign. But Mike Capstaff had seemingly vanished.

If he could get a lead on the owl-hoot, it might be possible to gather a posse and ride after the man. Or, alternatively, he could go after the outlaw himself.

But no information was forthcoming. Jack returned to the office, dissatisfied.

He was out in the street to meet the afternoon stage when it rattled in from Abilene. Judge Tarrant was an elderly man in black city clothes. He had a round, bald bullet head and a graven expression that never altered.

A party went along to the sheriff's office. There was Jack Griffin, Judge Tarrant and Trick Grant, the man he had brought along. Bertram Wast was present, with

45

an adopted air of interest becoming to a leading citizen. Doc Turner and Al Bride, as important men in the town, were present, too. They had been along to see the stage and, interested in the affairs of the town, had come along to the office.

Trick Grant was a tall, broad man, with gunman stamped indelibly in his every movement. He was dark-haired, with a touch of grey. His face was coarse and tough as leather. If he had been a sheriff, the town had evidently been full of outlaws, thought Jack.

He looked at Trick Grant's hands. The fingers were clean and supple. They were not the hands of a range waddy. The man had not done a day's hard graft for a long time.

Judge Tarrant was accustomed to speaking with authority, and he began to address the meeting.

'Gentlemen, we are aware of the unfortunate death of Sheriff Tom Mortimer. The murderer will be brought to justice. And for that Green Coulee, as a driving township, needs a new sheriff. As you know, I have the power invested in me as senior judge of Abilene County to swear in a new sheriff. I propose, therefore, to appoint Mr Ted Grant, better known as Trick, to the office of sheriff. Can we agree on that, gentlemen?'

Before anyone could utter a word in approval or protest, Jack Griffin drawled:

'I'm agin it. I want a vote from the people. I figure we should go to the people and ask them who they want for a sheriff. And if yuh want to know why, it's because I aim to be sheriff.'

There was a dead silence for an appreciable time.

46

Judge Tarrant looked nonplussed. His eyes sought Bertram Wast's as if seeking advice. Jack intercepted the glance, and his mind worked busily.

'If anyone objects to the appointment, then he can legally claim an election,' said Judge Tarrant slowly.

'I'm the hombre who's objectin',' said Jack firmly. 'An' I figure an election is a fair and square way o' settlin' the matter. I admit I have a hankerin' to be voted sheriff. At the moment, I'm holding the office of deputy. It ain't enough. If I was sheriff, I'd need a deputy – and I could swear him in.'

'That's so,' said Doc Turner, nodding his head. 'It's all the same to me. Maybe a vote is a good thing. What d you say, Al Bride?'

'Shore. Let's have a Green Coulee man elected,' jerked the storekeeper.

'You're wastin' your time, Griffin!' rasped Bertram Wast. 'Maybe you won't' get elected.'

'Maybe,' said Jack quietly. 'Anyway, I got to say there's nothin' personal against Trick Grant becoming sheriff o' this town. It's just that I figure I might make a better job o' it.'

There was an air of reluctance and indecision about Judge Tarrant. For a man who was accustomed to making quick judgements, he seemed momentarily stumped, and once again Jack noticed him glance quickly and interrogatively at Bertram Wast.

It was Doc Turner who made them act.

'Wal, if we are going to have an election, let's get going,' he cackled. 'Always plenty o' fun at an election. Some folks get drunk an' some folks get all shot!'

'Sure,' said Al Bride. 'We can hold elections any

time. Joe Blade's got a printin' press that can knock off'n enough voting slips in a few hours. You'd better start making some speeches, Jack!'

Bertram Wast seemed to make up his mind.

'All right, Trick Grant will put up for sheriff in opposition, naturally.'

'Why naturally?' retorted Jack.

'Because there may be some hombres who figure differently, Griffin,' said Wast softly.

With the decision, the men stamped out of the office and went different ways. Bertram Wast went with Judge Tarrant to the Packhorse Hotel, and Jack watched them go with a slight smile. The way he figured it, Bertram Wast must be pretty clever to be able to influence an Abilene judge.

It was pretty obvious that Wast wanted Trick Grant as sheriff. And just as obviously, Trick Grant had orders and understood them.

Doc Turner and Al Bride, as dutiful citizens of Green Coulee, went off to set the election in progress. There would be a few hours delay while the slips were being printed on the hand press, and then the election would soon begin. In a rough and ready way, but with justice, the votes would be counted and the result made known that night.

Jack reckoned to make a speech just before the voting began. It would be brief. He was no politician. The people either wanted a sheriff or they didn't.

He went to the livery and saddled his roan. He had decided to ride out to the Round-O and inform Ern and Bandy Manners about the election. With a swift ride, he just had time to make it. In fact, either Ern or

48

Bandy could come to town and make their vote. But one of them would have to stay at the ranch, in view of the attempt to burn the place the other day, even though Jane and Fred Spiceland were there.

Jack Griffin rode out as the sun began to climb and assume its familiar brassy glare. Soon it would be really hot. He kept to the defined trail which led out of Green Coulee over the flat, Panhandle country. Over on the horizon was the blur of the foothills which marked Ern's spread.

After an hour he was alone in the mesquite and shale land. The steady clop-clop of the roan's hoofs drummed out steadily The trail passed the first of the buttes. The Round-O was far off to the right of these solitary buttes.

He was tickling the roan gently with his spurs when a shot rang out from the butte. He was passing the rocky sentinel with hardly a few yards separating him from the big mass of rock.

He heard the whistle of the slug over his head and knew it for a steel-jacketed rifle shell.

Jack swung into quick, galvanised action. He pulled his rifle from the saddle boot, and with the same swift motion flung himself from his horse. His actions occupied mere seconds. and even as he leaped from his running horse, another shell screamed over the roan's back.

Had he been in the saddle, the bullet would have sliced into his guts. The marksman had the range now.

Jack went staggering forward under his impetus. The roan, scared by the fire, pranced away. Jack flung himself forward, and with a rush slithered into cover behind a large boulder. He lay still for a moment, sizing up his position. The large butte lay ahead, concealing the hidden bushwhacker. All around was brush, mostly catsclaw and mesquite, with shale and clumps of grass. It was typical semi-arid country. Ahead were the foothills that led on to the small canyons and buttes. All this poor quality land skirted Ern's ranch. Ern would have a hard job to keep the brush at bay and not over-graze his sparse grass.

The attacker was silent. Jack decided to try him out.

He used the old trick of raising his hat on the edge of his rifle butt. The hidden bushwhacker fell for it. A bullet screamed across the rock at once. Jack kept well down, pursing his lips ruefully. Well, at least, he knew the man had not ridden away.

Jack knew he had to take the risk if he wanted to locate the bushwhacker. He had to look out, draw the man's fire, and return it.

On his very first peep out he saw a rifle poke from the side of the butte. He ducked back as the shot whined into the boulder and ricocheted with a scream like a tight piano wire.

It was a grim spot. He had an idea they were playing for keeps. The man ahead wanted him dead. There ought to be a reason, and Jack had a few sudden grim hunches.

The rock was baking hot. He knew this stalemate could go on for hours unless the bushwhacker rode away. He had the advantage of the large cover afforded by the butte. He probably had his horse hidden behind it.

Jack glanced sideways and noticed the shallow

depression just a few yards away. It ran like a shallow crack in the ground for a fair distance, and it curved found close to the butte. But the amount of cover it afforded was poor.

He determined to try for the slit. Maybe he could get nearer to the man.

Jack tensed and then sprang out. He streaked like a mountain lion for the shallow draw. The bushwhacker got busy. Shots followed each other rapidly. Shells spat at the earth around Jack, and one whistled in front of his face. Then, seconds later, he flung himself flat into the shallow crack in the earth.

Jack did not stop. Holding his rifle, he snaked forward on all fours with astonishing speed. He knew that as long as he kept flat to the bottom of the crack, the bushwhacker could not see him.

Even so, owing to the undulating nature of the ground, he evidently afforded momentary glimpses of himself to the man behind the butte, for, as he moved along the crack, bullets followed him viciously. But every one was yards off him. The man was merely snapping shots off.

Jack scrambled along the shale bottom of the crack with his head close to the baked ground. He hoped no rattlers were sunning there. He hoped the bushwhacker would not climb to the top of the butte. Because that way the man could get a bead on his victim in the shallow, twisting draw.

And then, after some minutes of grim forward slithering, Jack reached the end of the slit. The depression began to level out with the rest of the ground. Only clumps of mesquite were around him, hardly providing cover from a rifle shot. He had only to lift his head and the bushwhacker would have a target.

Within a few seconds of reaching the end of the crack, Jack knew he had to move – but quickly. The ambusher would guess he was at the limit of the shallow draw and would have his rifle trained on the spot.

And yet the butte was closer now. The mass of rock rose up from the bed of the land hardly twenty yards away. The bushwhacker was hidden on the left of the rock. The man was evidently a sticker. But maybe he just thought he had a good chance of killing his man.

And Jack Griffin knew the man did have a good chance, in fact.

It was a tough situation he had ridden into. And had he continued on the roan, the bushwhacker would have got him with the second or third bullet.

Jack moved the rifle up, held it with two hands against his hip. He tensed every muscle. He knew he had to get up against that butte.

There was a brooding silence all around. The sun was high and brassy. Nothing stirred. There were no cattle nearby, no other riders. He knew he was simply a man lying close to the earth for protection. Ahead of him, hidden, was an unknown enemy. It was grim and unpleasant to slap up against the stark fact that you did not know if you would emerge dead or alive from the next few tense minutes. He might spill his life's blood on the arid land – or it might be the other hombre.

Seemingly, they were playing for keeps!

Then he leaped out, as fast as the bullets that had leaped at him. Even as he jumped into the open, his own rifle began to bark. He ran and hugged the weapon close to his hip, firing as he sprinted forward.

Crack! Crack! Crack!

He sent a fusillade against the edge of the butte. It had the immediate effect of stopping the other man's fire. The man had stepped back into cover. Jack could not aim accurately as he ran, but he emptied his rifle at the spot ahead.

All the time he dug desperately at the shale. His long legs leaped for the wall of the butte. He made it just as his rifle clicked dully. He had emptied the chambers.

And then he was flat against the rocky surface of the towering butte. He marvelled that the bushwhacker's first bullets had not found him as he had leaped from the slit. The first leap forward had been the crucial moment. After that his own rataplan of fire had deterred the man from taking chances by exposing himself.

Jack knew the man was on the other side of the butte. The man knew he was close. The fellow was probably waiting for him to make a false move.

Jack breathed grimly, and silently reloaded his rifle. Inside him was a savage intention to go on, to press the job to a conclusion. One of them would die.

He was as tightly strung as a mountain lion stalking its prey. His mouth was a tight, thin line. His eyes were narrowed. His wits were racing round the problem of how to get the man.

He exulted in the fact that he was now on equal terms with the ambusher. He was no longer a man hugging the earth and breathing a prayer. He had equally as much chance as the other fellow – and the man had just the same opportunity as him.

'I'm a-coming tuh get yuh, hombre!' he mocked loudly.

He waited, hardly breathing. There was deep silence. Nothing moved. He might have been a crazy man talking to the silent butte. Then a voice, thick with anger, came back.

'Yuh talk too much, Griffin. Don't over-play yore hand!'

Jack thought he recognised the voice. His eyes narrowed as he concentrated on identifying it. There was savage hate in the voice, he realised. It was the hate of a man who is riled because he has been outsmarted.

Jack decided to compel the man to talk again.

'Maybe yuh'll tell me what yuh got against me, stranger?'

'Maybe! You kin go to hell figgerin' it out fer yore-self!' was the prompt response.

Jack did not reply, for two reasons. One, he had identified the man. He was sure it was Red Holbin who, only that morning, had ridden into town with Bertram Wast. He had heard Red Holbin speak many times before in the saloons. His voice was clear, cold, and crisp as ice. Second, Jack did not intend to talk any more, for he realised he might be giving his position away. At first he had spoken in the exultation of the moment. Now he was more wary. He had even figured out Red Holbin's position from his voice. The man was no more than twenty yards away, round the jagged curve of the wall of rock.

Swiftly, he realised that the man who got to the top of the butte first would have the drop on his enemy. He could look down over the edge or manoeuvre until he had his opponent at his mercy. The man below would have little cover.

Jack reached up for hand-holds. He hitched his leg up and began to climb, making not the slightest sound. It was a job requiring agility, and here he knew he had the advantage over Red Holbin. The man, ruthless and callous, was older than he. He was pretty sure Red Holbin could not climb the butte wall without making plenty of noise.

Jack stopped once to listen. There was the same silence as before. He reached up, lithely and soundlessly. He hauled himself up another yard, making sure that his rifle did not touch the rock. Then another yard of ascent. He was nearing the top.

He was grimly determined to kill. Red Holbin, working on orders, had set the challenge. It was not hard to guess whose orders Red was carrying out.

Jack pulled himself on to the loose surface of the flat-toped butte. There was brush growing here on this miniature plateau.

He walked forward slowly, step by step, taking care not to dislodge the loose shale. He came nearer to the far end of the roughly rectangular-shaped mass of rock. The butte was about twenty-five feet high. The mass of rock had been left by some freak of nature as the land subsided or erosion sank the rest of the land.

Then, suddenly, he was at the edge of the rock. His first glimpse of Red Holbin was somehow strange. The man was waiting, flat against the rock, behind a small abutment that would give him cover from any approaching man. He had his Colts withdrawn. He was listening, his whole body ready for trigger-work. He was a killer waiting for the other man to make the move. Then his guns would blaze lead, gambling on sheer speed to win.

For a second Jack stood. His face was set in hard lines.

'Red Holbin!' he called softly.

His voice was without humour or expression. It was merely a cold, resolute warning to the man below.

Red Holbin jerked. His guns flew upwards. His face contorted with sudden fear as he realised the game was harsh and permanent.

Jack shot from the waist with the rifle before the other man's guns steadied. He triggered once, twice, three times.

Crack! Crack! Crack!

Red Holbin lurched back under the crash of the slugs finding his body. He fell back from the shadow of the butte. He went staggering backward awkwardly, with an incredulous look on his face. His guns dropped from nerveless hands. Then, suddenly, he fell swiftly on to his back.

Jack climbed down. He heard the neigh of a horse and knew Red Holbin had been waiting for him. The man's horse was still ground-hitched in the cover of the butte. Well, he would not need the horse any longer. He needed a burial party.

The answer to the bushwhacking was pretty obvious.

Red Holbin had been ordered to kill because someone did not want Green Coulee to have Jack Griffin as sheriff.

There could be no other valid reason. No one else hated him enough to go gunning and risking his life.

And Jack could guess easily enough that Bertram Wast was the man who did not want him to be sheriff. Wast had sent his hired gunman to kill him. Wast had figured that was the only way he could be sure Jack would not win the election. Dead men could not stand for the office of sheriff.

Why did Wast want Trick Grant as sheriff of Green Coulee?

4

Enter Ezra Hide

Jack Griffin worked quickly to bury Holbin. He heaped shale and rocks over the body. He certainly did not intend to take it back to town. He was content in the knowledge that he had won the grim struggle. Red Holbin had been defeated by gunsmoke justice. Along with Jed Slacks, he was the second of Wast's hands to go.

Obviously, it had been known that Jack had ridden out of town. Wast had sent his trusted man out to ride quickly and get ahead to a spot where he could bushwhack the man who intended to be sheriff of Green Coulee.

With the body covered, Jack stamped off for his horse. It had calmed down and was nosing for grass a few hundred yards away. As for Red Holbin's horse, Jack figured the animal would return to the Bar-K in its own time. Wast would know the answer when the horse came back without its rider.

The more he thought about the ruthless attempt to get rid of him, the more he was determined to stand for sheriff. His plan to settle on a ranch of his own could wait a little longer, until he got to the end of this crooked work.

He rowelled the roan in order to make fast speed to Ern's ranch. Soon the trail skirted the broken country. An hour later he rode into the Round-O ranch yard and leaped to the ground.

Ern Spiceland was in the yard, mending the pole corral. Fred and Jane were sitting around simply passing the time of day.

As Jack walked up stiffly, they all turned with interest.

It was Ern who realised there was something amiss. His sharp eyes searched Jack's dust-coated face.

'Thought yuh'd like to know there's going to be an election in town,' said Jack. 'Judge Tarrant came in from Abilene with a hombre called Trick Grant who was all set to take over as sheriff, but I claimed an election.'

And he told them about Red Holbin.

'Yuh got yoreself in bad with Wast now,' observed Ern. 'Kin yuh figure any reason why he wants Trick Grant as sheriff?'

Jack rolled a cigarette with deft fingers.

'Nope. Can't rightly say why Wast seems keen to git that Grant hombre installed. But I've a hunch he's planned it all. He was mighty friendly with Judge Tarrant.'

'And I've a hunch Bertram Wast is behind the death of Tom Mortimer and his deputy!' said Jane quickly.

Jack searched her piquant face, saw the indignation there.

'But it was Mike Capstaff who shot Tom Mortimer and Sam Brant!'

'That may be so,' she said firmly. 'But I feel that Bertram Wast is at the bottom of it. It's a woman's intuition. I don't like Wast!'

Jack and Ern grinned suddenly.

'I kinda agree, Jane,' drawled her brother, 'but you can't pin things on a galoot just because yuh don't like him!'

'All we've got are a lot o' hunches,' said Jack. 'They're mighty interestin' and I got plenty myself. But I want something definite to pin on Wast. It's still all kinda vague. Did yuh git those cows hidden away, Ern?'

'Shore. Bandy is out right now, ridin' the spread to see if'n any hombres come this way.'

Jack smiled slightly.

'It looks mighty like as if Bertram Wast is waitin' until he's got a sheriff he likes before he comes lookin' for his cattle. Supposin' he had Trick Grant with him an' he finds those longhorns with the worked-over brands. Why, then, they might even put yuh on the end of a hangnoose and answer questions afterwards, Ern!'

'Yeah! Wal, he ain't findin' them! Bandy and me got them hidden pretty good. Those beefs are right back in the foothills now. It would take a week of searchin' around to find them unless they were powerful lucky!'

'That's fine. Yuh coming to town to vote? I've got to get back. I guess I've got to speak to the people o' Green Coulee. Guess they expect me to say somethin'.

Shore don't know what to say exactly!'

And Jack rubbed the back of his head as if confronted with a problem.

'Just tell the people you stand for law and justice to rich and poor alike,' Jane said quickly.

He saw the interest in her clear soft eyes. He looked steadily into them and saw the flush mount her cheeks. She was bronzed, clear-faced, and he felt he liked her a lot.

'I'll remember that,' he said. He repeated the words: 'Law and justice to rich and poor alike.' He nodded. 'That's just what I wanted. Thanks, Jane.'

He could not know it, but she thrilled at his sincere compliment.

'I'll ride in with yuh,' decided Ern Spiceland. 'I got a right to vote. Bandy will be coming back for chow pretty soon. I'll leave him a note, though that ornery cuss can't read much. I figger yuh'd better get back to the hotel, Jane.'

'Say, I'd like to stay out here and help Bandy,' exclaimed Fred eagerly.

'Please yoreself. I reckon Jane will be all right at the Packhorse.'

'The way you talk, you'd think I couldn't take care of myself!' exclaimed the girl with a laugh.

'Maybe this town is gettin' too lawless,' returned Jack. 'But I'll say this, Miss Jane, as long as I'm in Green Coulee yuh can call on me if anyone makes trouble for yuh.'

And once again their eyes met. There was a flush in her cheeks, and she turned away with a half-smile on her lips.

Fred Spiceland stayed at the ranch, so there was no need for Ern to find some simple words which Bandy could read. A few minutes later they rode out at a smart pace along the trail for town.

It was a good, lengthy ride back to the cow town, and when they finally entered the main street, Jack's roan was caked with dust and lather. He rode right to the livery beside the Packhorse Hotel and gave the stableman instructions to rub down and water and feed the horse.

Jane went into the hotel to change into more feminine attire. She had been wearing blue jeans and shirt. Green Coulee, striving hard to achieve an air of civilisation like the distant town of Abilene, frowned on women who moved around its streets looking like slim youths.

Jack and Ern went along to Joe Blade's one-man printing business to see what progress the printing of the voting slips was making. Doc Turner and Al Bride were busybodying around. It was the usual excitement that preceded an election and if the issue were not so serious, Jack might have found plenty to laugh at.

There were calls for him to make a speech. Reluctantly, Jack climbed to the verandah of the printing office and hammered on the rail with his Colt butt for silence.

'Folks, I'm not sayin' much,' he said clearly. 'Yuh know a town which is mushrooming like Green Coulee must have law and order, and for that yuh need a good sheriff. Yuh also know that Tom Mortimer and Sam Brant were murdered by an outlaw name o' Mike Capstaff. If I'm elected yore sheriff, I promise to git that hombre, even if it takes a long time. He'll git a trial, unless he figures to shoot it out first. I promise yuh law and justice for rich and poor alike. That's all, folks.'

He was about to climb down when he saw Bertram Wast ride up on the outskirts of the crowd. The rancher, in black suit and hat, sat his saddle and stared for a fleeting second at Jack Griffin.

Suddenly Wast spoke harshly.

'I'll take you up on that, Griffin. I figure Ern Spiceland's got cattle o' mine on his land – and don't tell me they're strays. I've been losing stock lately – so my foreman tells me. I want an investigation. As deputy, you went out to get Ern Spiceland under Tom Mortimer's instructions, but he got away from yuh. Now I see you two are mighty friendly. Can I ask you what you're going to do about this rustling?'

Jack knew instantly Wast was trying to stir up trouble, for the many ranchers and cowboys who were in town that day hated all forms of rustling.

Jack could guess, too, that Bertram Wast was coldly raging inside at Red Holbin's failure to eliminate him.'

'I've been to the Round-O and looked around,' Jack retorted. 'I can't find any evidence o' rustling. There's nothing but Round-O stock on that spread.'

He knew Wast was aware he was lying, for the man knew the over-branded cows were on the Round-O Range. Jack was enjoying the undercurrent of animosity. The more that was said, the more he could guess at Bertram Wast's motives. At the moment the lack of motive was puzzling.

'Is that so?' snarled Wast. 'Wal, I figure yuh're making a big mistake, Griffin. If you can't locate a few rustled steer,' I challenge yore capacity to deal with the problems of this town as sheriff. If it's of any interest to the folks of this town, I can say I'm supportin' Trick Grant. This man has a fine record. If he's elected sheriff, I'll get him to deal with the missing stock. And if the folks of this town are crazy enough to vote for you, Griffin, I'll take my men on to Round-O Range and deal with this rustling myself as soon as I find evidence.'

'Better not over-play yore hand, Wast,' said Jack loudly.

The rancher wheeled his horse and jigged it down the street. All at once a hubbub arose among the crowd of cowboys, storekeepers, cattlemen and others who had listened to the exchange of words.

Grim-faced, Jack stepped down, and the crowd dispersed. The actual voting was due to start at four o'clock. With a small population of voters, the verdict would be known a few hours later and the affair discussed over drinks in the saloons.

Jack felt pretty confident of his chances. He was known to the people of Green Coulee, and Trick Grant was not. Wast knew this disturbing fact. Apparently, he'd thought Jack would step down when Judge Tarrant brought the man over. Or maybe he had counted on a successful bushwhacking of Jack Griffin.

One thing which stuck in Jack's mind was the possible motive Wast could have for his moves. Why did he try to plant Bar-K cows on Ern's spread? If it was

64

because he wanted to crowd Ern off the land, why in Texas did he want the poor ranch?

Bertram Wast had arrived in town five years ago. Before long it was apparent the man was out for power. He had arrived as a stranger and, during a drought year, began buying land. He had taken up leases, filed claims on free range. Over the years he had become the biggest man from Green Coulee to Abilene. Now he had everything. Why should he try to get the Round-O?

Jack had been away three years, bounty-hunting. That was a grim pastime. Now he was back, wanting to settle down. But events were keeping him away from that pleasant idea.

During those three years Wast had gained in power. And just lately he had apparently begun to work for the Round-O Range. Undoubtedly, his waddies had tried to burn the ranch-house. The cows were obviously planted, if one accepted Ern Spiceland's word. And there was the question of the body of Jed Slacks, which had mysteriously disappeared from the sheriff's office. Then Red Holbin had tried to kill the man who wanted to stand for sheriff. It all added up. But to what?

Then how did the murders of Tom Mortimer and Sam Brant come into the score? Who had paid Mike Capstaff to do murder? And for what reason?

'Guess I'll get the answers sooner or later,' muttered Jack. 'An' even if I'm voted out, I'll work on findin' Mike Capstaff. Tom was a good feller, though I figger now he knew Wast's accusations were faked.'

Jack went along to the saloon with Ern. He was not

a hard drinker, though he could do his share of counter-leaning. But he felt he needed a drink.

'That snakeroo aims tuh stir up trouble for me!' Ern confided. 'All that talk about rustling won't do me much good in the town. I ought to go for him with a gun!'

'Don't try!' said Jack sharply. 'He's clever. He does-n't carry a gun. Leastways, I can't see one. He's an east-erner that hombre. Never knew a rancher that never packed at least one hog-leg.'

'Why the hell does he want to run me off the Round-O?' raged Ern, bright spots of anger in his cheeks.

'That's what we've got to find out.'

The voting began a little later, and for the next few hours Jack felt strangely restless. Jane and he stood on the boardwalk of the Packhorse Hotel and watched the crowds drift past. It was noticeable that many Bar-K hands were in town. In fact, the whole outfit seemed to be in. Jack could guess at their votes. They would have orders.

At the ballot boxes Doc Turner, Al Bride, Joe Blade and a few more reputable men of the town were stationed. It was a rough and ready election, but it would be fair.

Jack did not intend to reveal that he had killed Red Holbin in a fair battle. He would leave it to Bertram Wast to start anything.

It was hours later when the result of Green Coulee's snap election was known. The result was overwhelm-ingly in favour of Jack Griffin. He had a clear majority. He was, therefore, sheriff. It only remained for him to be sworn in before Judge Tarrant. Whether the judge would relish the task was dubious, but he would have to get on with it.

The swearing-in was done with curt ceremony inside the sheriff's office. Jack immediately turned to Ern Spiceland.

'How's about yuh being deputy?'

'I've got my ranch—' began Ern, surprised.

'Shore. Plenty o' deputies have ranches or jobs. It ain't a full-time job. I can call on yuh when I want yuh. Hows about it?'

There was a gleam in Ern Spiceland's bright eyes.

'Shore. Why not? Anyone got any objections?'

Judge Tarrant shook his head hurriedly. Doc Turner was present, but Bertram Wast, evidently raging at the verdict, was not there.

'It doesn't matter who's got objections,' stated Jack. 'As sheriff, I can swear yuh in as my deputy. Same as Tom Mortimer asked me.'

And in a rough and ready manner, they went ahead with the oath. It was a curt, business-like proceeding, conducted by men who knew the taking of office was no sinecure and was often a ticket to Boot Hill. Only men with a strong sense of duty undertook such jobs.

Jack pinned the deputy badge on Ern's flapping vest. He wore a sheriff's star on his own gabardine shirt.

'All right. Yuh can get back to yore spread. But sooner or later we'll git work to do!'

'Suits me. But let me buy you a drink, hombre,' joked Ern. 'Remember, I owe yuh somethin' for that crack on the head I gave yuh!'

They spent some time in the saloon, and various

rannigans congratulated Jack Griffin. Mostly, the men were decent hard-working cow-hands and ranchers. But a few of the Bar-K outfit were in the saloon, and their hard glances were an indication of antagonism.

Ern Spiceland set off for his distant spread, and Jack rode out some way, realising grimly that anything could happen.

When he returned to his office he spent some time making a reward notice. He was going to offer some of his hard-earned money as a reward for Mike Capstaff, dead or alive.

'I still got enough to buy me that spread later,' he muttered.

It was very real, that hankering to buy a ranch and settle down to raising a herd of Texas longhorns. But it would have to wait. When the undercurrent of crookedness was cleared away, then would be time to hand over to another man.

He was sitting at the rough desk before the empty cells, thinking they would look fine if only one or two were filled with the rannigans who had tried to fire Ern's ranch, when a low knock sounded on the outer door. Jack stiffened, wondering if he had imagined the noise. Then, when it was repeated, he got up, hand near holster, and walked to the door.

He opened the door to admit a dirty, whiskered man. The man shuffled into the office passage with a furtive manner. Jack stared at the man. He looked like a range tramp.

'Howdy, stranger! What can I do for yuh?'

'Yuh want to locate Mike Capstaff?' the man rapped inquiringly.

Jack stiffened. His eyes narrowed, flicking the man. 'Shore do, hombre. What is it? Spill it!'

'I jest got into town,' mumbled the man. 'Jest heard about Mike Capstaff shootin' up the sheriff. Mighty fine feller was old Tom. I've bin up in the hills lookin' fer gold.'

'Texas gold!' interrupted Jack, surprised. 'Never heard o' gold in Texas!'

The oldster turned bright eyes on the new sheriff of Green Coulee.

'That's what all the durned folk 'round here say! But they's too iggerant to know what's under their noses. I kin tell yuh there's plenty o' gold up in the hills – an' not far from this town. I've seen all the signs, but I've never struck a bonanza.'

Jack shook his head.

'Yuh're not likely to, old-timer,' he laughed. 'No hombre round here figures there's gold in the hills. But git on with yore story about Capstaff. What have yuh got to say?'

'I cut his sign when I was up in them hills. That's all. I seen him. He made a camp in a cave in a canyon. I watched him, 'cause I knowed him fer a bad hombre. I figure he's living up there. Maybe he hunts his grub. I dunno. I jest came away quiet like. Never thought no more about him till I hit town. Then I hear about old Tom being gunned. So I'm here, Mister Sheriff.'

'Reckon I'm mighty glad tuh see yuh,' rapped Jack. 'I want that hombre bad. Can yuh lead me to the canyon? What's yore name, old-timer?'

'Name o' Ezra Hide. Shore I can take yuh up – only it's mighty hard on a jigger to hit town after being out

69

in them hills fer weeks and then leave town right off again.'

'What d'yuh want?'

Ezra's eyes lifted brightly.

'Figure I need a drink. Dust out o' them hills gits in a man's throat pretty bad.'

Jack grabbed his arm.

'What about showing me the way up to the spot where yuh saw Mike Capstaff – tonight! If yuh want anythin' to drink, I'll buy yuh a bottle o' whisky an' another bottle when we get back.'

'Reckon yuh know my likes! It's the lookin' fer gold. Mighty thirsty work – an' I've bin in those hills fer weeks!'

Jack reached for his hat.

'You got a hoss, old-timer?'

'Nope. I take a mule along wi' me into them hills.'

'Then I guess yuh'll need a fresh cayuse,' said Jack. 'Come along with me. I'll get yuh a hoss and a bottle. How far d'yuh reckon it is to the cave in the canyon?'

'Mebbe forty miles – mebbe less. If'n yuh settin' off now, reckon it'll take all night to ride.'

'Reckon so,' agreed Jack. 'And it's pretty hard country once we get out o' the limit of the Panhandle. I'll need a fresh horse. Reckon I'd better rest the roan.'

He took the dirty, bewhiskered old-timer along to the livery stable and got horses. He had to roust out the stableman from the comfort of his cabin at the back of the livery. Jack led out a handsome steeldust gelding for himself and a bay-sorrel for Ezra. As Ezra had no saddle except the worn gear on his mule, which was hitched outside Jack's office, a saddle rig had to be obtained from the liveryman. Jack led the horses along to his office and rigged his saddle on to the steeldust gelding.

He stuffed some canned beans into a grub bag and tied it round the saddle horn. His ammunition belt was full, with steel-jacketed slugs for the rifle.

'Let's get goin',' he said grimly when all was ready.

He was leaving no notice for anyone. He did think of seeing Jane for a minute, and then he changed his mind. It would be a good idea if nothing about this venture into the night got around. There was Bertram Wast to consider. He might make a move if he heard about Jack Griffin setting of with the old prospector.

Jack sent the old-timer along with some money to buy himself the bottle of whisky. He had a good idea Ezra was dead broke. These crazy old prospectors were all alike. They were always wandering off with a mule, a rifle and some grub and high hopes of striking a bonanza. Personally, he did not believe for one moment that there was gold in the hills. There had been rumours, brought to town by drifters, about gold being found in the distant Guadalupes, but those vast, arid mountains were a mighty long way from the hills which fringed this edge of the Texas Panhandle. No, only an old crazy coot like Ezra Hide would figure to find gold in the nearby hills!

Ezra came back after an interval. Jack was impatient. But he did not want to be seen setting out with the oldster. He sent Ezra on ahead with the bay-sorrel. Then, after a minute, he rode out, seeking the back alleys of the town.

On the trail leading out to the west of Green Coulee, he caught up with Ezra. He rode alongside – a tall, erect figure in the saddle. He had donned gloves. He took one off and rolled a cigarette with the ungloved hand. He offered the 'makings' to Ezra. The old-timer chuckled and showed the bottle he had stuffed in the saddle-bag.

'I like likker. Can't stand that Injun habit!'

After a while, they cantered along the fairly even trail. A moon had started to climb the clear sky. It was cool, in contrast to the heat of the day.

The two men made good progress, taking advantage of the flat terrain. Jack had a good idea that the combination of night and rough ground ahead would slow the horses to walking pace.

He had no clear plan about dealing with Mike Capstaff. He might not even catch up with the owl-hoot. The man might have moved on. But he was determined to stick on the fellow's trail for as long as possible. Ezra Hide had afforded a lead which might be the end of the outlaws.

After two hours of steady canter, they rode the horses into the edge of the broken country. Ahead, the hills loomed black and dangerous for riding in the night.

Ezra seemed to be content with his bottle. He raised it frequently to his lips. He sang a cracked song about a stranger and a ravine full of gold. Jack grinned slightly. He judged the oldster to be as hard as nails. He'd still be sitting the horse when the bottle was empty!

They rode into the butte country well after

midnight. It was pretty eerie as they passed the masses of rock. There were deep shadows, and the horses picked a path nervously. From nearby ridges coyotes howled at the rising moon. Now and then there was a harsh cry from a night owl.

Ezra pointed the way from time to time. There was no trail. The horses slithered on loose shale and rode increasingly steep inclines and then descended into valleys and canyons where only cholla cactus and Joshua trees grew.

They were now many miles from the cattle spreads. Ern Spiceland's ranch, which was the only one to reach into the broken country, was far to the south-west.

All night the horses plodded on, climbing into the arid country. Now and then they spooked as something stirred almost beneath their feet.

Ezra sang crazy snatches of song. Jack watched him through grim eyes. For himself, he could sit the saddle for twenty-four hours at a stretch, until the horse beneath him wearied. Many times, on such expeditions as this, he had ridden on, grim and saddle-stiff. He was wondering now if Ezra would keep it up.

Towards dawn, Ezra threw the bottle away with a curse.

'We're gittin' purty near to that outlaw's cave,' he cackled. 'See thet hill? Wal, we ride round the bottom an' into a canyon. An' that's where I saw that rattler Capstaff.'

Jack eyed the oldster keenly.

'There's a reward for that hombre, dead or alive – but only when I get him. Are yuh going to ride into the canyon with me?"

73

'If'n I kin git a reward, you bet!' was the reply.

'Wal, if I've got to draw gun on him, yuh might get only half the reward,' drawled Jack.

Ezra chuckled.

'Now ain't that mighty shrewd o' yuh! But I ain't complainin'. I kinda liked Tom Mortimer. Any reward will shore suit me!'

Jack stared at the distant hill. There was no timber and probably no water.

'That catamount certainly moved himself well out o' town. Can't imagine what he finds to eat up here.'

'Only jack-rabbits – unless he's got a cache o' grub!' cackled Ezra. 'But don't yuh worry about Mike Capstaff. He figures no one knows he's here. An' he's only a day's ride from Green Coulee.'

'Yuh're right there,' muttered Jack. 'An' if he's hanging around it's because he figures Wast might need him again. The more I think o' it, the more I believe Wast hired that ranny to shoot Tom and Sam Brant. But I ain't got a mite o' proof.'

There was obviously some credible reason why Mike Capstaff was hanging around the territory. Most outlaws, with the murder of two lawmen against them, would have moved a long way off, possibly into another state.

So the owl-hoot was out here in the wilds, betting on the vast spaces to defeat anyone who came looking for him. But he had not reckoned on an old prospector cutting his sign.

Even if Bertram Wast had hired him to kill Tom Mortimer and Sam Brant for some reason, Wast could not afford the outlaw any sanctuary. So the in-bitten rannigan had ridden out into the arid lands to lie low like a veritable rattlesnake.

Jack and Ezra rode round the base of the hill and halted. The canyon lay before them. There were deep shadows caused by the looming walls on either side. The canyon bed was pure sand. Jack could not see any tracks, but the shadows probably hid many.

'We'll ground-hitch the hosses,' he said softly to his partner. 'Then we'll go along on foot. Yuh sure this is the right canyon?'

'This is it,' whispered Ezra. 'I bin in these hills many times. I never make a mistake in my bearin's, Mister Griffin.'

'All right,' said Jack. 'Let's move in. But leave it to me. I want to talk to that hombre. He's more valuable alive than dead.'

'Shore. I'll show yuh the whereabouts o' the cave. Durn my hide, only a snakeroo would want tuh live out here! Not as if the galoot was lookin' fer gold. Now thet would be some durned good reason!'

A mere thin smile flitted over Jack Griffin's face. He withdrew his Colts and walked ahead, hugging the canyon wall. There was a sombre silence. Even the coyotes had ceased to howl on the distant ridges. He knew the slightest sound would travel for miles in the brooding night.

For that reason, he stopped at every few yards and listened intently. Ezra was right behind him. They halted, straining for the slightest sounds.

They knew a man might sing out here in the vast, arid land. A man might have to sing to keep his sanity.

But there was not a break in the soft silence that lay

like a mantle over the deep, dark canyon.

Ezra pointed to an abutment of the canyon wall some twenty yards away.

He put his mouth to Jack's ear and whispered:

'That's the cave. Figger he's still here? Mighty quiet, if he is. No fire, either.'

Jack nodded, kept his eyes glued on the abutment. He thought he could see a slightly different variation of shadow on the canyon wall. But it was slight. If Mike Capstaff were inside the cave, surely he would have a fire going to cheer him up?

Jack moved along step by step. It was a question of easy does it. One clumsy footstep and a man might walk out of the cave mouth with guns flashing flame through the night.

But nothing hindered the two men. They were right up close to the cave after a number of stealthy strides. And then Jack smelled the acrid swirl of smoke drift to him. It was not a lot, but it was undoubtedly wood smoke.

A fire was burning somewhere. He could not see a glow of flame, but the smoke was drifting along.

Jack turned the edge of the cave mouth and walked in. His boots pressed softly into fine sand. He went on with guns held waist high and menacing. The moment he had turned the corner he had seen the red glow at the end of the tunnel-like cave.

A man was tending a dull fire, placing dry bits of brush around the small blaze. His back was to Jack. He was bending over the fire, damping the swiftly burning brush with bits of cactus stalk. The smoke rose to the high roof and drifted along to the mouth as if some draught operated.

Jack went another three paces and then said harshly:

'Don't move, Capstaff!'

The bending man almost started to wheel in the shock of the moment, but he suddenly froze. His breath rasped with a sudden intake. His hands hung limply, not moving but almost twitching with the impulse to whip towards his guns.

'I'm Jack Griffin, the new sheriff of Green Coulee. I'm here to get yuh for the murder o' Tom Mortimer.'

There was no response from the outlaw. But his head moved almost imperceptibly as he tried to look round out the corners of his eyes.

'Get his guns, Ezra,' Jack said grimly. 'An' I guess I don't have to tell yuh not to get across my sights!'

'Yuh don't thet,' came the old-timer's voice.

Ezra sidled along the cave wall and then stretched out his hand slowly for the outlaw's holsters.

'I don't have to tell yuh I'll drill yuh if yuh make a move,' rasped Jack.

Mike Capstaff kept his hands at a careful distance from his holsters. Ezra plucked the guns out one by one, and stuffed them in his belt. Then he moved away, careful to keep out of the line of Jack's guns.

'All right, yuh can turn,' snapped Jack.

Mike Capstaff lumbered round. His dark, deep eyes stared balefully at the sheriff. He was a big man, in a burly, clumsy fashion. His in-bitten nature was almost written across his tight mouth and hard eyes. He was a killer, and it was stamped on his face. If his body was ponderous in its movements, his hands evidently were able to fly with the speed of lightning to his guns.

'What the hell yuh want with me?' he rasped.

'I've just told yuh – I'm taking yuh back to town for trial for the murder of Tom Mortimer and Sam Brant.'

'They was fair fights!' growled the man.

'Wal, yuh can have the opportunity o' provin' that. But I want the satisfaction of hearin' yuh talk right now. Who paid yuh to kill the old sheriff and Sam?'

'I don't know what the hell yuh're talkin' about. I tell yuh we jest fought about somethin'.'

'Don't give me that durned hokus-pokus!' snarled Jack tiredly. ''I aim tuh make yuh talk, yuh ornery cata-mount! I figure Bertram Wast hired yuh to blast Tom Mortimer and Sam Brant. I want a straight answer. Did Wast hire yuh?'

'I ain't doin' any talkin'!' sneered the other.

Jack eyed the outlaw grimly.

'Shore! I can guess yore play. Yuh figure Wast might be able to save yuh somehow when we get yuh back to town. If I wasn't such a danged fool, I'd plug yuh right now, and save myself plenty o' trouble. But I want yuh to talk. An' yuh goin' tuh talk right here and now. I'm not takin' yuh back to town until I've got some infor-mation from you. Now why did Wast get yuh to kill those two lawmen? What's Wast's play?'

Mike Capstaff had recovered his confidence some-what, for he hooked his thumbs in his belt and laughed. He had a pretty nasty laugh, and Jack felt he hated it.

'Figger it out, Sheriff! How come yuh so sure I know anythin', anyway?'

Jack eyed the burly man grimly.

'Ezra,' he called, 'put some more brush on that fire.

I want more light. Then get yore guns out and watch this hombre.'

Jack waited until Ezra complied with his request. Light from the thrown-on brush illuminated the entire cave. Shadows danced on the walls. Ezra got out his guns and pointed them at Mike Capstaff.

'What yuh figger to do with this hombre?' he chuckled.

For answer Jack pushed his guns back into his holsters. He did not take his eyes from the whisker-stubbled face of the outlaw.

Then Jack began to unbuckle his gun-belts. He worked quickly, but without undue haste. All the time he was sizing up the man before him.

Finally, he flung the gun-belts towards Ezra.

'I'm a-going to skin the hide off yuh until yuh talk,' he said grimly to the outlaw.

5

Mike Capstaff's Last Trick

Mike Capstaff wasted not a second after he grasped the import of Jack Griffin's intentions. Hardly were the words out of the sheriff's mouth than the big man leaped forward and closed with his enemy.

If Mike Capstaff thought that his burly frame could beat the other man by sheer weight, he was soon proved wrong. For Jack stepped back and rammed two fists into the other's face.

Jack was pretty grim. He wanted to smash this man and make him talk. It was not just an idea. It was a grim desire to punish. It was possible that Mike Capstaff held the key to the trouble in Green Coulee.

His fists ground into leathery flesh. Once more the outlaw tried to hug Jack, but Jack moved sideways and let his fists ram out in a one-two-three-four sequence of blows that made the outlaw hiss. The man halted and swung his huge arms. Jack ducked, slammed passing blows into the man's body.

Then for some minutes they hammered away. Capstaff went back, staggering and cursing. He thudded against the cave wall. His hand reached down and grasped a rock. As Jack came moving in, the man threw the rock in his face.

By a startling swift jerk, Jack dodged the rock. It hurtled over his shoulder and shattered against the other side of the cave.

Then, despite the tiring night-long ride, he was swinging blows with savage force into the outlaw's face. It was like smashing fists against dry hide. The man could take terrific punishment. And his own arms were swinging vicious hooks.

More than once Jack took a jarring blow on the side of the head. He staggered, halted momentarily and then whipped out at the body before him.

The fight went on in the glare of burning brushwood. They were two machines whaling hell out of each other. Back and forwards they fought, with Ezra a grim-eyed old witness. It was a battle of fierce, iron-hard men. If it were possible to kill with bare hands, they would achieve it.

Jack had almost forgotten his original motive in starting the fight under the savage impulse to smash the other man to bits. But, in every little breathing space, he remembered the purpose of the fight.

Mike Capstaff tried a few dirty tricks. Jack did not consciously hate him any more for using such tactics. They were only to be expected of a man fighting for his very life. But Jack nevertheless clung to a straight-forward method of fighting. He had two fists and he intended to beat the outlaw with those only.

81

The chance to smash the other to pulp came when the outlaw was flung once more against the cave wall. Jack surged up close and doggedly pounded with fists that felt like buckets of sand. He had a dim idea that Mike Capstaff was weakening, but he could not consciously think about it. All he knew was that he had the strength to go on for a bit longer. And so he hammered right and left to the battered face that jerked before his imperfect vision.

He knew Mike Capstaff was sliding down against the wall. He did not think about it. He pounded a fist at the whisker-stubbled face. The effort of ramming out a fist was sheer hell. But he continued to do it. His right lurched out after his left and then again. Dimly he knew the other man's fists were futile waverings. His own bunched fists slashed through them once more.

Mike Capstaff collapsed. He slid down the wall slowly. Blood blotched his evil face. Jack stepped back, shook his head to clear the haze. His breath rasped in his dust-laden throat.

Unknown to him Ezra stepped up and emptied a drinking pan of water over his head. Jack's head cleared with the cold water streaming down his face.

He bent forward and grabbed at Mike Capstaff again. The man was beaten, but he was not unconscious. He was just a pain-filled man unwilling to get up.

But Jack hauled him up, saw the bestial expression in the dark eyes.

'Talk!' Jack lipped through a bleeding mouth. 'Why did Wast want Tom and Sam killed?'

'I – I – tell yuh I don't know.'

The words were rasped out viciously. Jack hit the

man hard on his bloody countenance.

'Yuh – must – know!'

'I tell yuh – I don't!' screamed the man.

'All right! Did Wast hire yuh to kill them?'

'Shore! Shore, he did. He said he wanted a new sheriff and deputy.'

'Why? Give!'

'He didn't tell me everything!' snarled the outlaw. 'All I got to know was that Mortimer and Brant wouldn't take orders. I had to get rid of Mortimer. First I picked a fight with Brant. Then I jest rode into town again. I found Tom Mortimer in the saloon. I jest triggered and got out mighty quick. There weren't many hombres tuh shake off. I jest lighted out fer these hills.'

'I figured Wast wants the Round-O land. D'yuh know anythin' about that?'

'Nope. Don't know a blamed thing!'

Jack stretched out a hand to Ezra.

'Give me a gun, partner.'

The old-timer handed Jack one of his Colts. Jack held it close to Mike Capstaff's face while he gripped the man's shirt with his other hand.

'Yuh goin' into town with us and yuh're going to talk. Make a false move and I'll shoot yuh. I shore figured yuh knew more than yuh've told. But never mind. Yuh can testify that Bertram Wast instructed yuh to kill Tom and Sam. That makes Wast an accessory to murder. That's plenty for me!'

He flung the outlaw against the cave wall, and then he stepped back and buckled on his gun belts. Ezra chuckled and looked inquiringly at the new sheriff of Green Coulee.

'We hittin' the trail back?' he asked.

Jack shook his head and grinned through split lips.

'Nope. We eat. Tarnation! Yuh can't ride all night and then ride all day on an empty belly. I've got some beans and I reckon this snakeroo has some grub cached. We set and eat, Ezra. But first we tie this galoot's hands behind his back!'

There was rope beside Mike Capstaff's saddle and bedroll which he had stacked at the back of the cave. The owlhoot's hands were made secure. Then Jack and Ezra set about getting some grub inside them. Ezra went out into the dark canyon and fetched the horses along. While he was gone, Jack used some water Mike Capstaff had cached. He used the outlaw's cans to heat the water. He also used some to clean up his face. There was blood on his hands, and he wiped that off also.

Then Ezra returned.

'Seen this hombre's hoss ground-hitched outside,' he observed.

'Figured it would be somewhere around,' said Jack briefly. 'All right, *segundo*, set and eat.'

And Ezra ate as though the whisky had given him an appetite! Jack went through the food, knowing that there was a long and arduous ride before them. They would ride through the heat of the day. It would be tiring, and yet with a prisoner there would be every need to be alert. The horses would need water, and they would probably find none.

Finally, Jack arose and jammed Mike Capstaff's hat on the outlaw's head.

'We're movin',' he said.

The big man moved out of the cave ahead of them,

while Jack brought his saddle along. In the short time they had stopped in the cave, the night had lightened. It was half dawn. The sky was faintly blue and the moon was fading into obscurity.

Ezra saddled the outlaw's horse. Under the point of a gun, Mike Capstaff was helped to mount. Jack was already in the saddle, a gun trained on his prisoner in case he decided there was a chance of spurring his horse and getting away.

But Mike Capstaff sat like a grim, brooding person. His low cunning brain was undoubtedly turning over many schemes. Jack could easily guess the trend of his thoughts. The man probably thought there was a good chance of Bertram Wast finding some way to help him escape before he got as far as a hang-noose party.

But Jack was just as equally determined that that would not transpire!

Finally as dawn began to break fully, the party rode out of the canyon. The horses belonging to Ezra and Jack were somewhat refreshed by the halt and the chance to nibble the sparse canyon grass, but all the same the night's ride slowed them considerably.

All during the next few hours, as the sun rose and scorched the semi-arid land, Jack thought grimly of his future plans. With a confession from Mike Capstaff, he would be bound to arrest Bertram Wast. That would cause a stir in the town. But he would go through with it in spite of any fight from Wast or his pals. All he would need then would be a statement from some of the Bar-K waddies that Wast had ordered them to over-brand Bar-K cattle with a Round-O brand and then he would have a tight case against the man.

But he was up against a powerful man. Wast was friendly with men like Judge Tarrant.

It led back to the insistent question. Why did Bertram Wast want Tom Mortimer and Sam Brant removed? Why did Wast, who was wealthy enough, want Ern Spiceland's poor quality land?

So far there was no satisfactory answer.

For hours the horses plodded on through the broken country, passing gullies and arroyos decked with a veritable forest of octilla, cholla and saguaro cacti. This was brush country, shunned by the cattle-man, the home of jackrabbits and rattlers.

Jack found water in the broken country. It was merely a hole of scummy water, more like liquid mud. The horses managed to skim some clear liquid from the pool. It was no use to the riders.

They plodded on, finding the trail that led to the foothills and the butte country. Mike Capstaff, riding in the centre of the single file cavalcade, seemed resigned to his fate.

They stopped when the midday heat brought out the stink of saddle sweat from their horses. They rolled to the ground and stretched their legs. Mike Capstaff got off his horse and squatted in the shade of a rock. He leered contemptuously when Jack wiped sweat from his neck with his bandanna.

Jack nodded curtly to Ezra, and jerked a finger at the heat-hazed distance.

'We're gettin' into the Panhandle. No shade there. Wal, another few hours and we'll hit Green Coulee.'

'Shore, sounds good. Reckon I'll git my other bottle then?'

Jack laughed.

'Yuh will, partner. An' a reward for helpin' tuh catch a wanted outlaw. If yuh want to help me more, I can use yuh for a while.'

'Shore will, Mister Sheriff. All I want is a grubstake so as I kin git back into them hills and look fer gold.'

Jack laughed again.

'Yuh're in the wrong territory, Ezra. Sure figure yuh ought to get up among the Guadalupes. That's the only place in Texas where yuh'll find gold!'

'Guess yuh're wrong!' rapped back the old-timer. 'I've seen the signs, I tell yuh. I aim to stick right here an' find me a bonanzo. Yes, sir. There's a lode round here somewheres. I seen the signs, I tell yuh!'

Jack shook his head and glanced narrowly at Mike Capstaff. The sneer on the outlaw's lips was an indication of his thoughts. Capstaff evidently thought old Ezra crazy, like all gold-mad prospectors. Months alone in the deserts sent them all loco in the end.

Later they rode over the Panhandle country. The tree-less water-less land stretched for miles in undulating grass, mesquite and shale. On the horizon was the town of Green Coulee, where the grass grew thick and sweet and the Bar-K owned all the range.

When they finally rode into town, the sight of the three riders brought folks from stores and saloons to crowd the boardwalks, staring at the outlaw. There were rough cries of approval from many throats. Many men had known and liked Tom Mortimer and his deputy. This was the man who murdered them. In a land where sudden death at the end of flaming Colts was nothing new, the thought of pure murder was grimly resented. Many a man might die in a fair fight, but a murderer had no sympathy.

Jack Griffin got his man behind the bars of a cell in his office. Horses had been sent on to the livery for a well-earned rest. Jack paced the office in a grim thoughtful mood for a little while. And then there was a knock on the outer door.

He found Jane Spiceland waiting to see him. Her clear eyes flicked rapidly over his taut frame, seeing the lines of fatigue, the cuts and bruises on his face.

'Mister Griffin, you need attention!' she exclaimed.

He grinned thinly.

'Maybe I do, Miss Jane. Yuh heard the news? Come into this room. I got a hombre in the cell who is no good sight for a lady.'

'I've heard about your bringing in Mike Capstaff. The whole town knows. My, but you need something hot to drink and eat!'

And like a woman, she busied herself with the stove. While Jack washed and spruced himself, she cooked food for him. He ran a hand over his chin and figured it was a pity he had not shaved. Women liked to see a man looking smart!

He came out of the office where the wash-basin was kept and sat down to his meal thoughtfully. While he was eating, Ezra returned. He had been seeing to the horses, and he had bought his bottle of whisky.

'Set and eat and put that bottle away!' Jack said sternly.

'Shore always figgered beans 'n bacon went well with likker!' mumbled Ezra.

Jack Griffin had his problems to puzzle out. His

next move was to confront Bertram Wast. But before he did so, he needed to have his evidence straight. The first thing was to get a signed confession from Mike Capstaff. It would have to be verified. Even if Mike Capstaff implicated Bertram Wast in the planning of the murders for some unknown reason, the accusation would have to be backed with some evidence. Wast, powerful and clever, would simply deny the accusation.

So there were more moves to be made in this effort to bring justice to those who flouted the law.

Jack and Ezra went into the office. Jane came along in spite of the fact that Jack wanted her to keep free of the whole thing. He began to draw up a confession for the outlaw to sign. As Mike Capstaff could not write much more than his name, it was useless to expect him to pen a confession in his own words, so Jack wrote out a statement and read it to the man.

'Is that right?' he asked, after he had read the statement. 'Wast paid yuh to kill Tom Mortimer and Sam Brant for reasons yuh don't know. That correct?'

'I ain't sayin' anything,' snarled the outlaw.

The humour went out of Jack Griffin's face.

'Yuh confessed to that back in the hills!'

'Yuh kin go to hell!' snarled Mike Capstaff. 'This ain't the hills. Yuh can't beat me up in this town. I got rights. I ain't sayin' anything an' I ain't signing no confession.'

And the man made a vicious lunge at the sheet of paper which Jack held. He missed it. Jack walked back to the desk.

'I might have known it,' he snapped. 'Hear that,

89

Ezra? Reckon yuh heard that ornery galoot 'fess up in that cave. Now he figures to act clever. Shore can guess what's on his mind.'

Jack walked slowly back to the barred cell.

'If yuh think Wast will help yuh, yuh can figure it out again, polecat,' he said slowly. 'Yuh'll swing from a cottonwood shore as yuh're a mangey rat. Think it over.'

Jack ushered the girl out into the other room.

''Guess the air in the office is kinda tainted,' he said.

There was nothing to do about the outlaw at the moment. After a talk which left him very pleased with himself, Jack saw the girl back to her hotel. He was not away from the sheriff's office for long. He was not taking any chances. He had left Ezra in charge.

When he got back he spoke to the old-timer.

'Are yuh too tired to do another ride for me, hombre?'

'Goshdarn it – no!' roared Ezra. 'Where'n yuh want me to ride this time?'

'I want Ern Spiceland. He's my deputy. I want some hombre to give me some new ideas. I reckon he'd be kinda interested to know I've got Mike Capstaff.'

'I'll go right now,' promised Ezra.

'Yuh'll find a roan in the livery. Tell the jigger I've loaned yuh the hoss.'

'Shore was born in the saddle!' boasted Ezra.

'Wal, git. I've got to sit here and see no galoot gets ideas o' freeing that cuss in the cells.'

The brassy afternoon sun was setting when Ezra rode out of town on Jack's roan. The old-timer rode like a proud rannigan as was befitting a proud horse that could tear up the miles. He went out of town in a cloud of dust and a rapid tattoo of hoofs.

Let alone, Jack went back to the office and made sure the cell was secure. He made another attempt to get Mike Capstaff to sign the statement, but the outlaw simply snarled back at him.

'Suit yoreself, yuh in-bitten cuss,' grunted Jack. But yuh're in a bad spot to be figuring out tricks!'

Jack had callers in the next hour. Doc Turner came along and peered at Mike Capstaff

'Shore reckon you'll swing,' he grunted.

Two other citizens walked in and stood staring at the outlaw, thumbs hooked in belts.

'A dirty coyote!' hissed one man. 'I seen him shoot Tom Mortimer. Yuh can call on me fer a witness, Sheriff.'

Jack nodded, watched warily. His visitors stamped out, probably on their way to the Red Pine or some other saloon to enlarge upon what they had seen.

Jack realised that Bertram Wast would learn that the outlaw had been captured. Wast would not like the situation.

Jack had some peace for a few minutes. He was making a report of the capture of the outlaw. Although he had been raised on a ranch, miles from towns, he had had a rough and ready schooling. Using a thick steel nib, he slowly compiled the report.

There suddenly came a furious banging on the outside door of the office. Jack rose quickly, pulled a gun and went to the door. An old man, full of drink, waved his hands in drunken excitement.

91

'There's a darn rumpus goin' on at the Packhorse!' he bawled. 'There's an ornery Mex in there a-shootin' up the place! Thet greaser is drink crazy! Shore shootin' up the place—'

Jack did not need the drink-fuddled oldster to tell him something was going on down at the Packhorse Hotel. He could hear the sound of shots and the crash of breaking glass. Jack gritted his teeth and glanced back at the office. He was in a quandary. Dare he leave his prisoner? He had almost decided that he could not when he heard the sound of a woman's scream. The cry sounded piercingly along the evening air, above the shots and confusion going on in the hotel.

Jack ran forward impulsively. The scream had been like a warning to his brain. He thought of Jane in the hotel. Maybe she was in the lounge, and maybe the crazed Mexican was triggering lead all around!

Jack did not stop to think. There just was not time for deliberate thought. He went down the road at a long-legged speed and only paused when he hit the entrance to the hotel.

He steadied, two guns in his hands, his eyes narrowed and searching with the speed of lightning. He sighted the leering drink-mad Mexican. The man was standing on the reception counter, swaying with alcoholic fumes, a gun in each hand. He was a dirty, swarthy individual.

There was a woman in a corner of the lounge, but it was not Jane. She was an elderly woman, probably the wife of a visiting cattleman. She was scared. She shrank to a padded seat in a corner. The Mexican emptied his guns all around the lounge and then stopped to load again. He was so drunk, he dropped shells as he tried to fill his guns again. But he got some in. All the time he was singing a filthy border song.

Jack walked forward.

'Yuh can get down, hombre!' he rapped. 'Get down, pronto!'

For answer the man whipped his guns round and triggered crazily.

Jack used only one gun. The Colt roared and spat flame. The Mexican teetered backwards from the counter, clawed at air for a second and then fell with a crash to the floor.

The Mexican's shots had gone over Jack's head. But they had been near enough. A slug that came any nearer was certainly lead poisoning!

Jack holstered his gun grimly. Faces appeared at the doors leading into the hotel lounge. Jack went over to the lady in the corner, and at the same time Jane Spiceland rushed forward to hold his arm.

'Oh, my goodness, are you all right?'

He grinned, held her hand for a brief second.

'Shore think so! This town is gettin' to be like Tucson in Arizona – full o' ornery gents and loco Mexicans.'

Then it snapped into his mind that he had left Mike Capstaff unguarded!

He stiffened for a second with the urgent thought. The girl wondered for a moment what was in the mind of this tall lean man with the wary eyes which could, nevertheless, crinkle in a ready smile.

Then, without a word, Jack turned and moved with long strides to the hotel door. He thrust through and went swiftly along the road. There was something nagging in his mind. He recognised the symptoms of an insistent hunch. Something in his mind said ...

He never finished the thought. He went into the office with big strides, flinging aside the door. He moved into the inside office. He went up to the cell and stared down at the body on the floor.

The very moment he had seen the man prone instead of sitting or lying on the bunk, he had known the worst.

He whipped out the cell key and unlocked the door. He went inside, gun in hand. He knew he did not need the gun, though he had whipped it out instinctively, for he had seen variations of this trick before.

But it was no trick. Mike Capstaff was not lying doggo, ready to leap up and attempt to overpower his gaoler.

The outlaw would never try another trick.

For someone had entered the office and shot the man clean through the head!

There was a round hole, red with blood, dead centre in the outlaw's forehead.

The killer had been able to draw a bead while the outlaw looked directly at him!

As Jack stood up, he knew full well the identity of the killer – and he also knew Bertram Wast had bested him.

With the confession unsigned, it would be difficult to pin anything on the rancher. Wast had stopped any possibility of Mike Capstaff implicating him in the murder of Tom Mortimer and Sam Brant!

6

Ezra Rides
Alone

There was no need to worry about the prisoner now.
Slowly Jack went over to his desk and folded the
unsigned confession. He put it in a pocket of his shirt
and buttoned it down. Then he went out into the
street again and headed for the Packhorse Hotel.

The manager had already summoned Doc Turner
to deal with the body of the Mexican. In fact, the hotel
staff were busy tidying up and removing broken glass.
Jack went up to the manager and drew him to one
side.

'Got any ideas how this jigger come to startin' all
this?' drawled Jack.

The manager, a small man with a dark suit and a
large moustache, whose name was Telson, shook his
head.

'As you know, Sheriff, we don't allow Mexicans in
this hotel. It's our rule. He just suddenly appeared,

95

full of drink. My goodness, it's a good thing I believe in insurance. This town is getting worse!'

'Shore is,' drawled Jack. 'Wal, I've got ideas, but with this hombre dead it don't mean much. Guess I was kinda impulsive. Maybe I should have taken this man prisoner.'

He strolled up to Doc Turner.

'I'm shore raising business for yuh, Doc. There's another corpse for yuh back in the cell.'

Doc Turner jerked his head.

'You don't mean—'

Jack nodded grimly.

This rumpus was set up just to get me out the way for a few minutes. I can't tell yuh more, Doc, because I've got mighty little proof, but Mike Capstaff was paid to kill Tom Mortimer and the deputy. An' the snake who paid Capstaff also killed him.'

'That's yore business, Sheriff,' muttered Doc Turner. 'For me, I'm an old man, and I'm mighty tired o' seeing dead men. Holy angels, I ain't getting any younger, and all I see are dead men.'

'Wal, just for the records, I can tell yuh I had to shoot a hombre out by the buttes the other day,' drawled Jack. 'I buried him there. The galoot's name was Red Holbin. He was laying for me. But I got him instead. Reckon yuh don't need me to tell yuh he was one o' Wast's hands. Anyway, yuh can put it down in them records yuh keep that the hombre is plumb dead. I figure Wast knows it, anyway!'

'Red Holbin, huh?' barked Doc Turner. 'Seems to me there's some mighty queer goings on! I'm not asking any questions, young feller. You can get on with killin' them all for me! Wast, huh! Never did like that gent!'

There was nothing to be gained by asking more questions, but Jack did go round the saloons in the hope of finding information about the Mexican. He wanted to know if anyone knew the man personally. He wanted to know who had been talking to the man before he went along to the Packhorse to raise the rumpus.

Griffin questioned the bartenders and told them about the Mexican. In the third saloon he found the bartender who had served the man.

'Thet hombre never did have any dinero,' said the man in a quiet voice. 'But he had plenty in the last hour or so. I jest slung them along tuh him. Never saw no other rannigan wi' him, Mister Griffin. He jest got mean and drunk by hisself.'

'Yeah, I figure he just went crazy,' said Jack tiredly.

He knew, of course, that that was not the truth.

'Yep, those Mexicans do go crazy. Can't figger where he got all thet dinero, all the same!'

As Jack went out into the evening air, kerosene lanterns were being lighted in the saloons. He walked along, knowing that the Mexican had been paid to create the disturbance while someone went into the sheriff's office and cold-bloodedly killed the outlaw.

As Jack reached his office, he saw Doc Turner with two men. The men had the body on a sling.

'Reckon you don't want him around as an ornament!' rapped the Doc. 'So we're takin' him to Boot Hill right now. Yuh want to witness a burial party?'

'Not durned likely,' retorted Jack grimly. 'I'm

mighty tired, Doc. Take that galoot away. I figure I'm shore finished with him!'

With Doc Turner's cackling laugh in his ears, Jack went into his quarters to rest. He was really tired, though if any emergency arose, he could drive his frame on for another twenty-four hours. But in the meantime he felt he was entitled to rest just like any other man.

But Ezra was late. Jack glanced at the big clock on the wall. What was keeping the oldster?

As if in answer to his thoughts he heard the stamp of feet on the boardwalk outside his window. He heard Ezra Hide's high-pitched tones as he argued about something.

Then Ezra and Ern Spiceland walked in the room. The old-timer pointed to Jack and turned dramatically to Ern.

'Kin yuh beat it! Takin' it easy like while I ride my skin offen!'

'Set down and get that bottle out!' growled Jack.

And the old-timer lowered himself to a wooden chair as if his joints would hardly bend.

Ern's bright eyes flicked the row of cells.

'Where is he?' he asked.

Jack looked up grimly.

'Capstaff's dead. I reckon they're burying the coyote now. A certain hombre walked in here and shot the jigger to hell.'

And Jack told Ern and Ezra all about the rumpus at the Packhorse.

'I wanted yuh to work on that owlhoot, Ern. Yuh might have made him 'fess up. But the hombre's dead now.'

98

'Shore seems like I've had my ride for nothin'. Guess I'll stay in town overnight. As yore deputy, what about letting me have some floor space in this caboose? I got a bedroll on my hoss.'

'Suit yoreself – unless yuh want to sample the comforts o' the Packhorse Hotel.'

'Lissen, hombre,' grumbled Ern. 'I can't afford luxury. I got a mortgage on my spread, an' those long-horns are plenty lean.'

'Yuh ain't got the grass up there,' observed Jack.

Old Ezra began to cackle suddenly. He lifted the bottle and gulped the raw liquid. He patted the bottle.

'He ain't got the grass. Ha! Ha! Ain't got the grass!'

'You loco?' drawled Ern.

Ezra shook his head and suddenly shut up. But he continued to shake his head as if inward thoughts amused him. Finally he fell asleep in the chair.

'Wondered when the old cuss would give in,' muttered Jack. 'Yuh gonna hit the hay, Ern?'

'Not yet. Figger I'll run over an' talk with sister Jane.'

Ern paused in his speech. He walked slowly to the door.

'Mighty fine gal is Jane.'

'Yep. Mighty pretty.'

'Got brains an' book learnin'.'

'Yuh're right, Ern' Jack laughed softly. 'Figure I got a chance?'

'Maybe yuh have. Yeah, mebbeso!'

'Maybe I'd have a better chance if I hung my guns up and bought that spread,' muttered Jack thought-fully.

99

Ern went out with a slight smile on his lips.

Jack locked the door and partly undressed. He got into the bunk and fell asleep. There was roaring activity in the saloons but he was bone tired. Ezra sprawled in the wood chair, the bottle of whisky on the table before him.

It was an hour later Jack had to open up again for Ern Spiceland's return.

'Set yoreself in,' growled Jack, 'and lock them doors. I reckon there's another day.'

'There always is – except for dead hombres!' drawled Ern.

For the rest of that night Jack Griffin knew no more. But from force of habit he wakened with the dawn. An hour later the three men were ready for a good breakfast. Like all good range men, they could fend for themselves.

'Jane is going out to the ranch with me this mornin',' said Ern. 'Yuh care to ride out? Unless yuh got business here in town?'

'Nothin' pressin',' answered Jack.

The sudden idea of riding along with Jane was appealing.

'I reckon to go over wi' yuh, Mister Spiceland,' yapped Ezra eagerly. 'I shore reckon to do that. Kinda like the looks o' yore ranch!'

'Yuh do? Then yore the only feller round here does! Exceptin' maybe Wast!'

They rode out of town slowly that morning. Jack had saddled his roan while Ezra, flush with money Jack had given him, hired a fresh horse. Ern had his own mount – a bronc from his remuda out on the ranch. Jane was riding a proud pinto.

Jack Griffin found he was able to ride alongside Jane most of the way. She looked charmingly wholesome astride the pinto. She was wearing blue jeans tucked into riding boots. She had a buckskin jacket over her red shirt. Her wide brimmed hat hid most of her corn-coloured hair. She was clear-skinned and yet bronzed. Accustomed to seeing the courageous women of Green Coulee riding side-saddle, Jack was impressed by Jane's capabilities. The women of the town mostly travelled by buckboard, but when they saddled a horse, they were hampered by their long skirts and had to ride side-saddle. Jack, impressed by Jane's modernity, felt pleased with himself and yet he realised there was no actual need for him to ride out to the Round-O.

He began to make excuses for himself.

'Reckon I'll see yuh to the ranch,' he said, 'and then cut across to the Bar-K outfit. I've still got to trace the hombres who worked those brands on the Bar-K cattle. Then I figure some blacksmith made the branding iron.'

'I don't suppose Bertram Wast borrowed Ern's!' she laughed.

He was thoughtful riding erectly, gloved hands holding the reins close to his waist.

'Nope. There's still a-plenty to do before I can pin anythin' on Wast. And yet I'm sure that ranny is up to no good. Capstaff confessed that he was hired by Wast to kill Tom Mortimer and Sam Brant. That's enough for me, but not enough to rig a trial. An' with Wast being so powerful in this county, I've got to have an iron-hard case to put up.'

101

'You work with law and order,' she remarked.

'That's so. Mighty easy to pick Wast up and go for a gun – but that's not law. I can guess he sent Red Holbin to git me, but I can't pin anythin' on Wast because the other hombre's dead. Same with the attack on Ern's spread – one galoot's plumb dead, and it would be mighty difficult to prod the other rannies into speakin' against Wast.'

'But you'll clear this business up,' she said coolly.

He turned his head.

'I intend to do just that, Jane. An' then maybe get myself that Box-T spread. It ain't fittin' that a man should go around with a gun against other men all his years.'

'You want to ranch out here?' she asked softly.

He looked directly into her clear eyes.

'Yeah. It seems to me a man should get himself some roots. An' this is the biggest cattle land for miles. An', Jane, when I get that ranch—' He paused.

She looked away, at her horse's bobbing head. And then she turned to him again as if unafraid to show the soft light in her eyes.

'When I get that ranch,' he said awkwardly, 'I'd shore be pleased if yuh would come over an' tell me how yuh like it. Because that's mighty important.'

'Is it, Jack?' she said softly.

'Yeah. Mighty important.' He gulped. 'Because I reckon to build it the way yuh like it.'

There was a shining glow in her eyes now.

'I'll be over, Jack,' she murmured, 'to tell you how to build it.'

The sun climbed steadily and blazed like a furnace.

The trail was well used and dusty. Cattle herded in the distance of the undulating land of mesquite grass, shale and sand. To Jack Griffin the problems of the sheriff's office fell away and the ride was momentarily magical. His thoughts about the Box-T spread crystallised. He had to get this job finished and set about digging in his roots!

They brisked the horses to a canter and kept it up until they reached Ern's ranch. As they rode into the ranch yard, Bandy Manners and Fred Spiceland came to meet them. The four riders climbed down. Ezra led he animals to the feed corral.

'You know somethin'?' bawled Bandy. 'I seen Bar-K riders up in the hills this morning.'

'Were they on our range?' asked Ern curiously.

'Yep. They didn't see me. Wast was with them – an' that ramrod Otto Tribe. There was two other hombres.'

'What were they up to?' asked Jack.

'I figger they bin lookin' for those longhorns!'

And Bandy nearly doubled up with laughter. He was wearing sheepskin chaps, and he slapped them with a horny hand.

'Them jiggers won't find them cows! I got them hidden in a canyon – take more'n a morning o' ridin' to locate them cows!'

Ezra Hide strolled up and heard Bandy's last remarks.

'Mebbeso they weren't lookin' fer cows,' he yapped.

Bandy Manners had met Ezra last night and was now fully acquainted with the eccentric old-timer. As a matter of fact, the two men were similar types, except

103

that Bandy had spent his life herding cattle and Ezra had drifted to searching for gold.

'What in tarnation would those rannigans be lookin' fer?' demanded Bandy.

'Mebbeso yuh were right,' said Ezra hastily.

'Crazy as a coot!' muttered Bandy. 'Sure is one thing about cows – they don't send a galoot crazy. Plenty o' sense in cows. Kin eat 'em, too!'

'It would serve Wast right if I herded those beefs round by Abilene and sold them to the railroad crews working out there,' snapped Ern. 'I could git them round by the hill country an' then across the Panhandle without touchin' the Bar-K Ranch. Shore would serve him right if I made some dinero out o' them cows!'

'But yuh're not going to do it, Ern,' Jack said quietly. 'Those beefs are evidence – when we get the fellers who did the branding or maybe the blacksmith who made the iron.'

'Shore. I was only talkin'.'

Jane had entered the ranch-house. Jack watched her go. He was about to follow, with the idea of talking about the desirability of a good ranch-house, when he felt Ezra tug at his sleeve.

'I bin thinkin',' said Ezra, fingering his whiskers thoughtfully. 'Yuh treated me right fine, an' I'm an old man. I figger yuh ought to ride along with me.'

'What in tarnation are yuh talkin' about?'

I reckon yuh oughta ride out wi' me,' insisted the old-timer. 'We kin go up to them foothills where the butte country starts.'

'We shore could, but we're not,' retorted Jack.

104

Ezra sighed and attempted another track.

'Kin yuh tell me if'n that broken country lies in the Round-O title?'

Jack leaned back against the pole corral.

'Shore it does, but I don't rightly know the borders. Reckon Ern could tell yuh. What's on yore mind, old-timer?'

'Nuthin', much,' said Ezra rapidly. 'Let's go see Ern.'

Ern was round by the side of the ranch-house, inspecting some new carpenter work Bandy had done to the burned timbers. Ezra and Jack strolled up.

'This old feller want to know about yuh borders in the broken country,' declared Jack.

Ern turned and grinned.

'Since yuh ask, old-timer, I'll tell yuh. I got title to the land that extends ten miles into that cussed country, an' I wish there was as much grass out thar as there is in the Bar-K Range. Nothin' out there but canyons, buttes and brush. Can't help figuring that the brush is gonna spread someday right down to this range. Can't feed cattle on cholla cactus and catsclaw.'

'How come yuh got all thet land?' inquired Ezra.

'Why, it was in with the title. Had to take the lot or leave it. Guess it must ha' been passelled up that way when the Injuns sold it to the Administration. Anyhow, if yuh really want to know everythin', I've got my title deed with a copy lodged in the County Courthouse at Abilene. An' there's stakes out in the broken country showing my borders. I put them stakes there myself. Should be there now.'

'Yuh sure told me everythin',' muttered Ezra.

He rolled off and hitched one old leg on a rail of a fence, and stared at the blurred hills in the distance. Heat was hazing up, distorting the view.

Jack grinned at Ern.

'Queer old feller, but I like him.'

'Shore. He can stick around here, if'n he likes it. Can't pay him, but I've got plenty of grub.'

But Ezra suddenly decided he would go riding alone. He went to the feed corral and got his horse. It was already saddled. There was a rifle stuck in the saddle boot. With a wave of his hand, the old-timer spurred his horse out of the ranch yard.

As Jack Griffin stood by the rail and watched old Ezra spur his horse out across the land, he felt a queer kind of inward hunch. It was not so much mental stimulus; there was a disturbed feeling in his stomach. Too late, he realised he had not really questioned Ezra about his reasons for urging him to ride out to the butte country on the outskirts of Ern's land. What was really behind the old-timer's many questions about the ranch's borders?

And then the inward hunch resolved itself. It became a hard, startling question in his mind. The disturbed feeling left the pit of his stomach; his brain was grasping with ideas.

All the same, Jack hesitated; for the ideas were preposterous. Ezra was touched by the desert sun. It was no use taking any account of his cracked ideas.

And yet, as Jack stared at the tiny dot which was Ezra on the horizon, he felt he ought to go out after the oldster.

After all, the fellow had asked him – and then

apparently got tired of asking. Ezra, following his lone tactics, had ridden out alone.

Suddenly, Jack turned and walked swiftly to Ern.

'I'm a-goin' out after that ornery old buzzard,' he called. 'Don't rightly know why. Give my regards to Jane – but I'll be back soon as I shake some sense out of that old jigger's head.'

'Yuh'll have a hard job doin' that!'

Jack got his roan from the corral and trotted the horse out of the ranch yard. He set off at a good canter across the country.

As he rode, he noticed the poor quality of the grass and, in fact the downright lack of it. There were many patches of shale, and Ern was right – there was too much brush. Even now cholla cactus was springing up among the shale where the mesquite grass would not flourish. Cholla cactus was bad. Too much, and the land would be covered in a few years. The grass would die as the cactus roots drained all the moisture – and there was not much moisture at any time.

But soon his thoughts swung to Ezra again.

He had lost sight of the old-timer. Apparently Ezra had rounded the first of the buttes. But Jack had a pretty good idea of the general direction. He rowelled the roan into a faster gallop.

He rode fast over the ground, the steady drum of hoofs hammering out. Without slackening speed he rounded the first butte and then urged the horse still faster towards the rising broken ground ahead.

He could not see the old-timer. He would have to sight him soon if he wanted to talk to him now and not return to the ranch after a senseless ride.

Jack had to slow to read the track. He could not see Ezra or his horse. But he located the cayuse's hoof-prints in the sand of a small canyon that rose into the shale hills ahead.

He rode on for some minutes, wondering if he should throw the whole hunch aside and go back to the ranch.

Then he was suddenly alert as a shot rang out!

Jack was suddenly still in the saddle, his boots pressing hard against the stirrups. Even as he tensed for further sounds, there was a perfect rataplan of shots from ahead. He judged it was mostly rifle fire. He rowelled his horse instantly. The animal sprang forward along the canyon.

He heard no more shots. Had any rifles barked from ahead he would have heard them above the drum of his roan's hoofs.

Jack urged the horse up the shale slope. He breasted the ridge and rode full speed down the other side. The horse slithered and was wide-eyed. The incline levelled out into another canyon of irregular shape, and at the distant end a dark blotch sprawled on the virgin sand and a horse cantered in uncertain circles.

Jack knew the sprawled figure was Ezra. He sent the roan up the canyon in a burst of speed and flung himself off the horse before the animal slithered to a halt. He felt sure the attackers were not around. He leaned over the old-timer and turned him round.

Sharp breath hissed in Jack's mouth as he saw the spread of blood on the oldster's shirt. Taut lines dragged in Jack's face as he realised the old fellow was dead. The bullet was plumb centre on the heart. No one could live with that type of wound. He tried a few tests and then sat back realising the futility of it.

He stared grimly at the canyon walls, an unspoken curse in his heart against the unknown men who had killed Ezra. He jumped to his feet and his hands fell to his gun butts. He crouched, wishing some enemy would appear so that he could kill him!

But there was no sign of man in the arid hills. There was only the brooding silence which was the eternal feature.

The men who had killed Ezra were a long way off. He could not hear or see them.

Jack dropped to the body of the old-timer again and brooded over the tragedy. Why had the old fellow been killed? Who had killed him?

He could make a darn good guess as to the identity of the attackers. Bandy's remarks about seeing Bertram Wast and his hands in the hills that morning was a good hint. Had Ezra fallen foul of Wast and Otto Tribe? Had they shot him?

If they had, the next question was – why had Ezra been killed?

True, Ezra had helped Jack to capture Mike Capstaff. Maybe Wast had extracted revenge. That could be it.

But Jack felt dissatisfied. Some hunch, nagging in his mind, told him that Wast would not identify himself as a murderer before his men, no matter how much he trusted them.

There was something else.

Jack lifted Ezra's body with the intention of placing it on the horse's back. He noticed the way the old fellow's hand was grasped around a large, chunk of rock. Curiously, he placed the body down again and gently removed the rock from the clenched fist.

It was some few seconds before the importance of his find struck Jack Griffin; and then, in a flash, it was all clear.

He knew enough about gold-bearing quartz to see that this piece of rock was so filled with wire and flake gold that slivers of pure yellow metal could, without too much difficulty, be pried out of the stone with a knife!

This, then, was Bertram Wast's aim and pivot of all his nefarious plans!

7

Gold Canyon

It was all so clear now. Wast wanted to chase Ern Spiceland off his land so that he could step in and buy it without raising suspicion. Just to make continually higher offers would have the effect of making Ern suspicious because there was no ordinary reason why Wast should desire the Round-O land.

So Wast had settled to worrying Ern in the hope that he would give up trying to raise herds on the poor land. Wast had sent his men to fire the ranch. Wast had thought of accusing Ern of rustling. Any of these measures, had they succeeded, might have sickened Ern into selling and getting out. Once Wast had the title to the land, he could file claim to all the gold-mining rights. In view of the richness of the piece of quartz Ezra had clutched, it seemed that the lode was on the Round-O land. This valueless territory which Ern had title to was, therefore, potentially rich. No one suspected that there was gold in the broken country so near to the edge of the Panhandle. The very idea was laughed at. Texas was a cattle country, except for the uncharted and dreaded Guadalupes far to the west.

Jack Griffin sat still over the body of his old partner and brooded bitterly on the irony of Ezra dying with the coveted gold within his grasp. All his life the old-timer had sought gold. Probably it had been a craze with him. And he had been right about the signs of gold which his expert eyes had detected in this broken country so near to Green Coulee.

Why had Wast killed the old-timer?

There could be no other reason than that the lode was somewhere nearby and that Wast had seen Ezra acting suspiciously. Ezra must have been fairly sure of the location because he had ridden straight out from the Round-O to this canyon. He had asked Jack to ride with him. The old-timer had wanted Jack to examine the canyon. Apparently Ezra had been through the canyon last night, when he went out to seek Ern. Maybe that was why Ezra had been late in returning.

Jack sighed. Everything was necessarily conjecture, but some things stood out. Ezra was dead and beyond aid. There was gold in this country and on Ern's title. Bertram Wast knew it and apparently desired to corner the wealth.

Probably Ern Spiceland's title deed gave him mineral rights to the land in his borders, though maybe Ern never had thought about that when signing the deed. Few men would have given the idea serious consideration, for the general opinion of the broken country was that it was arid and useless.

Jack rose swiftly, conjecture dropping from his mind. He had to get Ezra back to the ranch. He had to talk to Ern.

He carefully pocketed the quartz and then placed Ezra's body across the roan. Jack got to the saddle and rode forward, stopping to pick up the reins of Ezra's horse. Then, with the other horse on lead, he cantered out of the canyon.

After a fairly slow ride he came within sight of the Round-O buildings squatting flat on the Panhandle country without so much as a cottonwood for shade. When the winds came, as they did every year, Ern would have to stake his ranch-house to the earth with ropes.

Jack soon attracted attention, and before he reached the ranch Bandy Manners and Ern came riding out furiously. They had seen the riderless horse.

Jack' explained it simply.

'Wast. He or his men shot Ezra. Found him in a canyon. He'd exchanged shots with some rannigans afore a bullet got him. Got somethin' else to tell yuh, Ern, but it'll keep till after we bury Ezra.'

'Thet ornery polecat!' roared Bandy. 'D'yuh figger to let Wast git away with this, Sheriff?'

'He won't get away! But when I say it was Wast, Bandy, yuh got to realise I never saw the galoot shoot Ezra. I've still got to work for proof.'

'Doggone blasted bushwhacking skunk!' roared Bandy, incensed and helpless with the knowledge that there was nothing he could do to help Ezra now.

They rode into the ranch-yard, and Jane and Fred came out. The girl was suddenly white and shocked

113

when she realised what had happened. Little muscles twitched in Fred Spiceland's jaws.

'It's murder!' he exclaimed in a low voice.

Jack was a tall, lean, foreboding figure as he glanced sternly at the others.

'Wast won't get away with it. The hombre will reach the end o' his trail pretty soon!'

They had questions, but he evaded the issue. There was a simple, stern, yet necessary job to do. Ezra had to be buried with his small worldly goods.

Jack recited a few words of service over the grave they dug. He had performed this task before in his travels with rough, iron-hard men who had lived and died out on the trails.

Ezra's grave, out in the open country, was marked with a heap of stones, and then they left.

'Yuh've asked a few questions,' said Jack gruffly. 'If yuh'll come into the ranch-house, I'll tell yuh something mighty important.'

Rather mystified, they all walked quietly into the small living-room of the ranch-house. They sat down, finding seats with difficulty for there were only three chairs.

'I reckon yuh're all interested in Ern's success with the Round-O,' began Jack. 'Bandy, yuh're Ern's *segundo*, and I know yuh're with him. Fred and Jane – yuh're Ern's brother and sister. So here goes.'

He brought out the piece of rock and laid it on the table. He smiled slightly at their puzzled expressions. They just stared at the rock and then looked up at Jack. Their movements were so much in unison that it was rather comical.

114

Ern was the first to reach out and scrutinise the quartz closer. After no more than a few seconds his jaw tightened and his bright eyes flicked across Jack's face.

'Where'd yuh get this, Jack?' he asked hoarsely.

'I didn't get it. I found it in Ezra's hand when I reached his body. Know what it means, Ern?'

Ern Spiceland's eyes were eagle-sharp.

'That's gold, ain't it?'

He tried to pick out a sliver of pure yellow metal with his thumb-nail. The flake of gold curled out and Ern put it on the palm of his hand.

'It ain't fool's gold, is it?' he asked stiffly.

Bandy just stared at the quartz rock. Then: 'Yuh don't mean to tell me that old feller found gold round here?'

'He talked last night about gold,' said Ern slowly. 'I – wal, I – I – figgered he was kinda loco about the subject.'

'He wasn't so loco. D'yuh know what it means, Ern? I found this rock in Ezra's hand. He was shot dead in a canyon inside yore land. He was shot by Wast or his rannigans, shore as thunder. An' he was shot because Wast knows about this gold. Knowin' about the gold is the only goshdarned reason why Wast would want to squeeze you outa this ranch. Yuh got the title deed to a bonanza, Ern. An' Wast wants yuh out so he can buy yuh up without raisin' suspicions. That hombre wants power. He's not content with the wealth of his ranch – he wants the untold wealth of gold!'

There was a hushed silence, and they all stared at the chunk of rock. Except for the streaks of yellow, it might ordinarily have passed notice.

115

'I'm no expert,' said Fred Spiceland, 'but if you believe this is gold, it explains all Bertram Wast's actions. Let me see your deed, Ern. Guess I'm the only lawyer around here!'

Ern jumped up. He went to a closet and brought out a strongbox. He unlocked it swiftly, whipped out the parchment deed with the spindly, copper-plate writing.

Fred read through it carefully but with expert ease as befitted one who was studying law. After a few minutes he said slowly:

'You've got clear title to all minerals inside your land. Ordinarily that would mean just the right to a lot of rock and shale. Wast must have guessed this clause was in your title.'

'Unless he has seen the copy deed in Abilene,' put in Jane quickly. 'Mister Wast is very influential – look at the way he is so friendly with Judge Tarrant.'

'Could be,' remarked Fred. 'Of course, Wast could make a bargain with you, Ern. Knowing that there is gold in your lands doesn't show you where to find it. Wast could have made a bargain and shared the gold with you.'

'That doesn't suit a big hombre like Wast,' drawled Jack. 'That buckeroo wants the lot. Sharing is not his code. It's not in that hombre's character to figure this business out honestly. He's the sort o' galoot who wants more and more power, an' squeezing yuh out is just the sort o' thing he would think about.'

Ern rose to his feet and paced the room. He walked back and forwards over the skin rug.

'D'yuh figger the gold is in that canyon, Jack?'

'Seems mighty like it.'

'Then we'll go find it. Then I'll fence off the claim and set up camp there. Wast won't beat me down. An' yuh're all in on this find. We split whatever we git outa it. I only wish that old hombre was alive to git a few bottles outa it! Anyway, even if we don't find the lode, I shore wouldn't sell to Wast for a fifty-fifty! The gold kin stay where it is, afore I'd benefit thet coyote!'

'That's yore best plan,' agreed Jack, rising. 'Get a camp up there. Gold spells trouble anyways. Plenty o' bad hombres get movin' around when gold is heard of. An' it'll get around. Yuh'll need guns to protect yore property, Ern. There'll be other rannigans beside Wast.'

'I'll take care o' that,' growled Ern. 'Now I know the whole set-up. Wast won't beat me. Not if I knows it!'

Jack handed him the lump of quartz.

'It's yore's,' he said.

Ern Spiceland laid a hand on his arm. His eagle-bright eyes scanned Jack's lean, grave face.

'I tell yuh, yuh're in on this. Yuh were Ezra's last pardner.'

'I'm the sheriff, Ern. Reckon I was just doin' a job.'

'Maybe. But yuh can be sheriff and pardner in this gold bonanza, too.'

Jack smiled.

'All right. Figure I'm just as human as the next hombre. But yuh got to find the lode first.'

'Let's git goin',' said Ern.

He looked round the room impatiently and frowned at Jane.

'I'm not so sure about yuh, Jane. Guess yuh'd better

stay here with Fred. Guess we'll be hungry enough to chow a whole leg offen one o' them beefs afore we get back.'

'Maybe,' she retorted, 'but I'm going with you. I want to see this gold too. I can cook enough to feed you men when we get back.'

'All right,' growled Ern. 'But maybe Bandy an' me will be stayin' up in them hills – if we find the lode. Yuh'll jest have to ride back to that padded hotel in town. Can't stay out here. Maybe Jack will ride back with yuh?'

And Ern threw a smiling glance at the girl.

They moved out into the ranch-yard, and for the next fifteen minutes they were busy loading two pack-horses. They loaded stakes, timber, wire and nails on to one horse. The other carried enough canvas to rig a tent, rope and a box containing sticks of dynamite.

'Never know what we'll want!' muttered Ern.

The party of riders set off eventually, and only when they were riding out did Ern Spiceland realise that he was leaving the ranch-house and buildings unattended. He cursed.

'Thet darned coyote! Fine thing when a jigger can't leave his home unguarded for an hour or mebbeso!'

He had to decide to risk it.

The ride into the canyons was not a fast journey, for the pack-horses merely trudged along. But presently Jack led the way over the shale hill and down into the long canyon where he had found Ezra lying. The memory of it made his lips tighten.

And then they reached the spot where Ezra had fallen. Jack pointed, and the others realised the significance of his gesture without need of words.

'I figure Ezra would have us look for the gold,' said Jack. 'That old hombre tried to get me out here. Shore wisht I'd gone with him!'

Jack began to scan the tracks around. The others sat on their horses while he studied the sign. He was looking for track of Ezra's last footsteps. He moved far away from the centre of the canyon floor and found tracks of a horse with a man's footprints alongside. The tracks led from the canyon wall to the centre of the wide canyon – right to the spot where Ezra had been bushwhacked. Jack was moving against the direction of Ezra's tracks. The sign brought him right up slap against the rocky pileup of the canyon wall. There were fissures and cracks, some of great depth, at the bottom of the canyon wall. The ground, too, was rocky and the tracks faded out. But Jack found enough evidence of Ezra's last trail. The old-timer had ridden his horse parallel with the canyon wall, skirting it all the way. Then he had moved out into the centre. Jack wondered why. Was it because Ezra had found the quartz?

The others were still three hundred yards away, in the middle of the canyon. The sand was brilliantly white under the glare of the sun. They were keeping off the tracks because they did not want to confuse the trail.

But Jack waved them over. He stood by the spot where Ezra had departed from his hitherto unwavering attachment to the canyon wall. He was looking down at the deep fissures that ran jagged at the bottom of the wall. They were volcanic in origin, he knew. Like all men who had pioneered the western trails, Jack knew something about gold. He was not the old gold-hound that Ezra had been; but he had more than a smattering of gold lore. He knew, for instance, the difference between fool's gold – a bright mineral ore – and the real thing.

The others rode swiftly over the white sand. The party dismounted, dropping the horses' reins over their heads so that they were thus ground hitched as the reins trailed on the canyon floor.

'I'm a-goin' down one o' these fissures,' declared Jack. 'Figger yuh can tackle the others, Ern. It's yore gold – if we find it!'

'We'll find it, right enough,' stated Ern Spiceland.

He climbed down the jagged crack in the floor. The depth of the fissure was fully fifteen feet. As he scrambled carefully down the slit, he examined the rock. So far it was just red-stone. Slightly disappointed, he reached the bottom and stood on the bed of fine sand that had blown into the crevice during the years. He made a careful examination but for the life of him he could not locate any quartz that resembled the chunk Ezra had picked up. He worked along the fissure to the far end and scaled the wall again. There just was not any gold bearing quartz in sight. This could not be the place from where Ezra had obtained his rock.

Jack climbed out and shook his head to Fred, Jane and Bandy. Even as he walked down the canyon wall to another fissure, he heard the yell that rose from the crevice into which Ern had climbed.

'Jack! Git yoreself down hyar!'

Jack stared over the fissure at the figure of Ern as he

120

scrambled along the bed of the crack in the earth. Then, infused with the other's excitement, he rapidly climbed down the deep cleft and joined Ern on the bed.

The fissure was sand and rock and pebbles. Immediately he noticed the bright gleams of yellow in the rocks around. Wind and rain had burnished the streaks of gold, and the metal was easily detected. But Ern was holding a handful of dull pebbles and stammering with excitement.

'This is gold, goshdarn it! Yuh kin jest rake the nuggets up! The bed o' this fissure is thick with 'em!'

Jack took some of the pebbles. With a thrill that he could not disguise, he scratched the pebbles and saw the gleam of virgin gold. The pebbles were nuggets!

He bent down and scooped around in the bed of sand. Within seconds he had a handful of rocks and nuggets. Quickly he discarded the rocks, even though some had evidence of flake and wire slivers of gold. The remainder of pebbles were pure gold nuggets, he soon ascertained.

'It's a bonanza!' he exclaimed hoarsely. 'Hey, Ern! There's a fortune in this gash! Who would ha' believed it! There's enough gold in this placer lying around to be scooped up to make the lot o' us rich for life.'

'Yuh're durn right!' yelled Ern. 'I figger yuh don't even need to dig fer the stuff.'

'Ezra must ha' found the lump o' quartz in this gash,' stated Jack. 'Wast or his men must have seen him gettin' out o' this cleft They didn't figger Ezra held the secret in his hand even if he was dead.'

Ern straightened his shoulders.

'Let's take it easy, Jack. This gold kin wait till we set up camp. I figger Jane ought tuh git back to town. Ain't so good for her to be up here.'

They climbed out of the steep-walled gash. The others were waiting for them at the top and sharing their excitement, for they had heard the exclamations.

Jack and Ern showed the other three the nuggets.

'Jest swept 'em up!' boasted Ern. 'This placer is a natural!'

'Won't need no dynamite!' laughed Jack.

'It's unbelievable,' breathed Jane, as she stared in fascination at the handfuls of small nuggets. 'Is that really gold? I'm sure I don't know.'

'Shore it's gold! Yuh jest scratch the nugget!' Jack explained. 'An' here's the real test!'

He took one of the nuggets and placed it on a flat stone nearby. Then he rummaged for a hammer in the packs.

He began to hammer the nugget. After a few strokes, it became flattened. He hammered away with deft taps and the gold assumed a flat shape. He beat it out until it was no thicker than a Mexican dollar.

'If it's malleable, it's gold,' he said with conviction. 'Fools' gold won't beat out. Too brittle. Shore, this is gold an' plenty of it! Yippee!'

They broke into a babble of excited conversation. It was Jack who stopped the whole thing dead.

'Git those pack-hosses into cover!' he shouted.' Git behind these rocks – everyone! There's riders at the mouth o' the canyon!'

They all wheeled and stared for a brief second at

the horsemen riding fast up the sandy bed of the canyon. Then Ern and Bandy wheeled for the horses They grabbed rifles from the saddle boots. They pushed the horses into a natural stall in the canyon wall. The horses went into the little, rugged high-walled enclosure. The foot of the canyon wall was littered with large boulders. Within second the thoughts of everyone were switched from the fascinating lure of gold to the menace of the approaching riders.

For even from a distance, they could distinguish the big, black-suited form of Bertram Wast. He was astride a big all-black horse. Beside him was Otto Tribe, and behind them were two other men.

'Gold and death!' thought Jack. 'Shore is a true saying!'

When the horses were safely in the little gulch and Jane was sent to keep them from being spooked, Ern, Bandy, Fred and Jack dropped behind the big rocks. They had rifles at the ready. Fred Spiceland gulped, realising the law of the gun was as powerful as the law of the pen.

The approaching riders suddenly wheeled their mounts on their haunches and went off at a tangent across the canyon bed. They were making for the other side of the canyon.

'Seen us,' snapped Jack to the others. 'I figgered they weren't takin' much notice as they galloped up.'

Wast led his men to the other canyon wall, and they found cover just like Jack and his friends. Even so, Jack could see movements of dark-coloured men and horses against the red stone canyon walls. He figured the targets were nicely in range. With a rifle, he could reach them. But the same thing applied to Wast and his hands.

There was silence in the canyon for an appreciable moment.

'I wonder what that snakeroo figgers on doin'?' jerked Jack to Ern, who was sprawled behind the boulder hardly five feet away.

'Guess he'd like to kill us all,' retorted Ern. 'That sidewinder must guess we've found the bonanza.'

A hail from the other side of the canyon alerted them.

'Griffin – I know yuh're there! Why don't yuh come out and take yuh rightful place on the side o' law and order?'

Jack raised his voice.

'What in thunder d'yuh mean, Wast? Speak out, feller!'

Bertram Wast's strong voice came back:

'Yuh siding with rustlers, Griffin. Don't know if you rightly know it. But my hands have been ridin' all morning, and they've found Bar-K cattle hidden on this Round-O spread.'

'Yuh don't say? Maybe strays, huh?'

'Nope. These cows were re-branded – and I haven't sold any cattle to Ern Spiceland. They're rustled stock, Griffin. I want yuh to do yore job. Yuh got to arrest Spiceland and that side-kick of his. They rustled my stock. That clear, Griffin?'

There was a muffled curse from Bandy Manners.

'A pisen snakeroo! Found them beefs! Doggone polecat! Iffen I could git a bead on him, he wouldn't call me no rustler!'

Jack smiled grimly.

'Cut out the bluff, Wast!' he shouted clearly and coolly. 'I know why yuh're here. I know about the beef. I'm collectin' evidence. If yuh're worried, the case will be settled in the proper time. Until then, I'm not arrestin' anyone for rustlin'. If yuh want to know, I'm lookin' for a murderer!'

'I figure yuh got your loop tangled, Griffin!' shouted Wast. 'For the last time, I give yuh the chance to work with me. Hand Spiceland over, or we come and get him. He's a rustler, and I've got the proof.'

Bertram Wast's scheme was pretty clear. He wanted to get rid of Ern, so that the Round-O would be put up for sale by the County administration when Ern failed to pay his mortgage dues. Then he would step in.

Maybe he intended to kill Ern and claim that he had gone for his gun when accused of rustling. If he got Ern out of the way, he could point to the worked-over brands on the cattle as proof of Ern's guilt. Whatever happened Wast had circumstantial evidence to back his actions. The fact that it was framed evidence need never come out.

'I've told yuh, Wast, I'm handlin' the law around here!' shouted Jack. 'I'll decide about those cows. An' don't get too clever. I've told yuh, I'm lookin' for a murderer. Yuh ain't foolin' nobody, Wast. I've got good ideas where to look for that killer.'

There was silence and then Bertram Wast's voice snarled back:

'All right! Let's quit foolin'! Yuh know what I want. Yuh not even as smart as Tom Mortimer and Sam Brant. I got them under my thumb. They took money from me. But they didn't work fast enough at gitting Spiceland off this land, an' then they wanted to back out. Mortimer signed yuh on as deputy. I reckoned he was goin' to blab. Wal, he didn't – and neither did Sam Brant. Even when Brant was dyin', he didn't get no chance to talk to anyone but Mortimer an' me. Old Mortimer was too dumb to guess what was coming to him – or he'd ha' talked to yuh!'

Jack levelled his rifle round the boulder. He sighted grimly. But there was nothing to fire at. One thing he was sure about, Wast would be good as a dead hombre!

'I'm a-coming to get Spiceland!' shouted Bertram Wast. 'And if anyone gits killed, it's sure too bad. If yuh all git killed it won't worry me none – and the folks in town don't like rustlers.'

'I reckon they don't like murderers either!' Jack flung back across the expanse of silent sand.

Wast had some sort of case to put forward if anyone in Green Coulee got bold enough to challenge him. Wast could say that Jack Griffin was helping Ern to flout the law. And as for Bandy, Jane and Fred, they were Ern's friend, brother and sister. If they were killed, Wast could claim they fired on him as they helped Ern to resist arrest. Wast could say he intended to arrest Ern himself and that Ern resisted and got killed in the shooting. In fact, Wast could put forward a pretty smooth story if needed, and although it might look suspicious nothing could be proved or disproved. And Wast could step in and buy the Round-O if every-one were out of the way. The key to his whole story was the planted beef, and the man had discovered the cattle apparently. That was why his riders had been seen by Bandy early that morning.

Although it had not so far been mentioned, Bertram Wast must realise that the gold had been discovered, for they were hiding almost on top of the bonanza. For a moment Jack wondered why Wast had taken Otto Tribe into his confidence – and the other two men. But evidently Wast had bribed them with promises of riches if they played the moves his way. Only the men would never live to share the gold with Wast. When their usefulness was over, they would be eliminated. Wast would emerge as the only controller of the gold.

'Reckon that's lookin' a long way ahead,' muttered Jack. 'An' it wont' come off!'

The parley was over. A rifle barked from the opposite wall of the canyon and the steel-jacketed slug tore into the rocks beside Jack.

Jack flattened out on his stomach and poked his rifle round the boulder. He peered out and thought he saw a black patch show against the lighter colour of the canyon wall ahead. He sighted his rifle and pressed the trigger. The dark patch disappeared.

Rifles spoke from both sides of the canyon as the men fired in their grim eagerness to blast someone out of this world. Jack was guilty of a few shots at dubious targets. Then he realised that the battle could go on for ever until one side was spent up with regard to ammunition.

Bullets whined into the boulders, spurting dust and chips of rock into the air. The horses were spooked by the sudden gunfire, but June was able to soothe them.

Bandy triggered into the fleeting targets on the other side of the canyon and then started to curse and reload.

'Shore ain't nobody goin' tuh git killed here!' he muttered loudly. 'Those hombres are only stickin' thar noses out them rocks. Can't hit a nose at this distance nohow!'

Jack grinned, twisted his head to see that Jane was all right. He was anxious about the girl. Jane was a schoolteacher. A shooting party was no place for her.

'Reckon yuh're right, Bandy,' he called out to the broad, little man. 'Guess we could keep this up till nightfall – unless yuh would like to stick yore haid out and test them hombres' aim.'

'Me? I still got plenty to live for!' growled Bandy.

'I've got an idea,' said Jack slowly.

Ern moved his head and looked at him interestedly.

'Wal, we won't decide anythin' this way. Maybe we'll just use up all our shells, or maybe we'll be forced to ride out when it's sundown. But we've got some dynamite.'

'Yeah? What yuh got figgered?' demanded Ern.

'Just this. Two o' us could climb the canyon wall and get on to the top. Nacherally, Wast will see us – maybe shoot. That's a chance we've got to take. There are plenty o' rocks to flop down behind, and I reckon we could do it. We take the dynamite with us. Get it?'

'Nope,' growled Bandy. 'But I shore reckon I'll take that climb wi' yuh!'

'All right, I'll explain,' said Jack. 'We take the dynamite an' climb to the top o' the canyon wall, an' then we move around to the head o' the canyon – iffen

128

Wast or his men don't git us with a slug. But once we git to the top, we've got plenty o' cover, I reckon. Once we hit the head, we move down on the other side o' the canyon till we're right above them hombres. That's being lucky, I shore admit. Then we throw the dynamite down among them galoots. Shore will be kinda rough on 'em! If they run for it, they'll be a good target from this side o' the canyon.'

'How come I can't think o' ideas like that! exclaimed Bandy. 'Let's git thet dynamite, Mister Griffin. I'm a'goin' with yuh!'

Jack glanced interrogatively at Ern.

'Is it all right? D'yuh mind stayin' here with Jane and Fred? Or maybe I should? Kin Fred shoot straight?'

'You bet I can!' exclaimed Fred indignantly.

'Suit yoreself, Jack,' said Ern. 'It's yore idea. I kinda like it. Two guns can keep those hombres off. They won't come over the canyon bed. I wish they would. I'd git them.'

'Right. I'll git along with Bandy.'

'Is this strictly lawful?' inquired Fred Spiceland with a laugh.

Jack flung him a smile.

'Shore ain't. But this canyon ain't Green Coulee, an' something has to be decided right here an' now.'

He slid back carefully from his position at the rock and jumped the last two yards which separated him from the small gulch which sheltered the horses. A second after he reached Jane, a bullet ploughed a spray of sand after him. Evidently Wast's hands were really alert.

The boxes of dynamite were still packed on the pack-horses. It was certainly a good thing that the canyon wall afforded plenty of shelter. The jagged, irregular walls which rose from the sandy bed provided a multitude of hideouts. The dynamite was sheltered from all but a thousand-to-one chance ricochet.

Bandy made the jump from his rock to the little gulch, and as sure as salt a bullet whined after him, too! But Bandy was in shelter by the time the marksman had sighted.

They opened the boxes of dynamite. In all they had ten sticks fitted with fuses.

Bandy and Jack hid them inside their shirts. Grimly they buttoned up again.

'Kinda messy iffen a bullet hits 'em!' muttered Bandy.

'Shore be a quick way out!' said Jack.

Before they started on the climb, he took Jane's hand for a fleeting second.

' 'Bye, Jane. We'll teach those hombres somethin'!'

'They might shoot you!' she whispered.

He knew about the possibility, but he shook his head and smiled.

'We're quicker than mountain goats!'

Bandy and Jack took their rifles along as a precaution, although they were an encumbrance in climbing. Ern watched them, and as Jack reached up for the first foothold in the jagged wall he said to Fred:

'Keep up a rataplan! We'll keep those jiggers behind rock till Jack and Bandy hit the top.'

Fred and Ern began firing, not wildly but methodically. The idea was to keep Wast and his hands behind rock.

Jack went up the wall as fast as he could. When he had got a few yards start, Bandy came after him. Jack went on, heaving himself up the rock face, expecting bullets to whistle near him. There were many footholds and hand grips. And then he found a narrow ledge that slanted steeply upwards behind a diminutive wall. He scrambled up like a goat. He heard the fusillade caused by Ern and Fred below. Then a bullet pinged into the rock ahead of him.

Some marksman had chanced the rataplan set up by Ern and Fred and had moved out of cover sufficiently to take aim at Jack. But the bullet had gouged the rock ahead.

Jack looked backwards. Bandy was coming up pretty fast.

So far so good. But the top of the canyon wall was still a long way off.

Jack moved all the time. If the men over at the other side were prepared to take chances to get him, he would have to keep moving. He took advantage of every bit of cover and more especially so when two more steel-jacketed shells whined almost in his face.

He heard other shots and knew they were directed at Bandy. All the time Ern and Fred pumped lead out over the canyon. A grim battle was in progress.

It was still grimmer to realise what would happen if Bandy were hit. For if a bullet went anywhere near his shirt, the heat of its passage would detonate the dynamite. Jack would soon know if Bandy stopped a bullet anywhere near his body.

Jack's boots were not so good for climbing. The high-heels slipped sometimes on the loose shale. But he moved upwards all the time, and he gulped for breath with the speed of his climb.

Then, suddenly, he moved on to the top and immediately threw himself down behind some rocks. He waited for Bandy to appear.

The old-timer suddenly came up like a goat. Jack grabbed him, dragged him forward. They fell behind the rocks in a heap.

'Hey! Yuh ought tuh be careful wi' this dynamite!' protested Bandy. 'This stuff kin go offen with friction.'

Jack drew in a deep breath.

'Right! We've made it. We'll keep below the rim of the wall all the way round. Wast might think we've gone for help if he don't clap eyes on us. I don't figger he'll guess we've got dynamite. With a bit o' luck, he won't think we're movin' round to his side o' the canyon.'

'Not until we blow him tuh hell!' muttered Bandy.

8

Canyon of Death

Their progress was swift, now that they could keep below the ridge visible to Wast and his hands. The gunfire in the canyon below died away. Ern had guessed they had reached the top safely.

But it was a longish trek round to the head of the canyon, and the rocky plateau had no trails. Bandy and Jack ran most of the time, leaping from rock to rock, dodging down gullies thick with cholla cactus. The ground was baking hot after the day's sun. They disturbed a few basking rattlers.

'Figger we could collect a few o' them sidewinders an' drop 'em on Wast's rannigans,' exclaimed Bandy.

'Fine. But mebbe the rattlers wouldn't pisen their own relations!' returned Jack.

They plunged on, safely below the ridge of the canyon wall. They reached the head and turned the rocky bridge of the blind canyon. They moved on

133

steadily, grim now that their destination was nearer.

Bandy wiped the sweat from his neck, looked doubtfully at the bulge inside his shirt.

'Hope yuh don't git too hot!' he muttered.

Jack Griffin led the way down the table-land of rock He heard a few desultory shots from the canyon. Evidently they were still exchanging shots. He was not unduly worried about leaving Jane. He could not see how Bertram Wast or his hands could approach Ern or Fred across the canyon bed without asking for trouble. The situation down there was a stalemate unless one party decided to ride out. Even then they would have to run the gauntlet of the other party's fire.

But he cast aside conjecture. The facts were plain and ominous for Wast and his outfit.

Jack and Bandy came nearer to the spot where Wast and his hands were hidden. Jack took a few rapid glances over the rim of the table-land to get his bear-ings. He could see Ern and Fred's position clearly. Ern was firing from time to time. Smoke curled out from the rock which marked his position. It was hard to realise that it was a grim stalemate down there. They were not playing; it was a grim game, with death the jackpot.

There was not much need to hide from the edge of the table-land now, for the Bar-K men could not see above them. Jack jerked a hand to Bandy to join him, and they peered over the rim of the canyon wall.

'This is the place,' said Jack.

The canyon wall was sheer. The drop to the bed was about one hundred and fifty feet, Jack reckoned. At the bottom was a mass of jagged rocks parallel to the wall. In the cover of the rocks Wast and his men and horses lay hidden.

'That ranny hasn't guessed what we're doin',' said Jack. 'Maybe he thinks we just got out in an attempt tuh get back to the ranch an' then git hosses.'

'Reckon thet's so,' muttered Bandy.

'If it is,' said Jack thoughtfully, 'he'll figure he ought to get out himself pretty soon. I'm mighty shore Wast doesn't want half o' Green Coulee to know his ornery plans. Even Wast can't fool everybody!' Jack stood on the edge of the canyon wall and brought out the sticks of dynamite from his shirt. He knew Ern would see him. He felt bitterly ruthless. He did not like the job. But Wast's threats were real. The man threatened death to others. He would have to accept what was meted out to him.

It was the law of survival.

Being a sheriff was nothing out in this wild, arid, merciless land. His power was only real when the majority of others in the community backed him. And right now there was no law or order in this canyon. There could be only gunsmoke justice.

'Light them fuses and pitch the sticks over, Bandy,' Jack ordered grimly.

Bandy had no scruples.

'Yuh darned bet I will!'

They lighted the fuses and watched them burn a little so that they would be near to detonation when they hit the ground below. There was no question of the fuses being extinguished on the descent.

Jack swung the first one over. Bandy followed suit. Swiftly they lighted two more and threw them down.

135

They were busy with another two when the first explosion came to their ears.

Jack and Bandy threw the remaining sticks over the canyon rim and crouched behind cover as the dynamite roared. They could not see anything, but the din was terrific. Jack knew the grim inward feeling which came to him whenever he thought of other men dying violently. He knew it would be a miracle if any of the four men survived the blast below.

When the noise had faded away and there was no chance of debris hurtling up, Jack walked to the edge of the canyon wall and stared down.

The mass of rocks below had been merely altered in pattern it seemed. He could not distinguish the difference, but he could see the shattered body of a horse. And then all at once his attention was jerked to the centre of the canyon bed.

Two riders were cruelly spurring their horses to the mouth of the canyon. Jack stared in sudden disbelief. One rider was Bertram Wast. The other – Jack narrowed his eyes – was Otto Tribe!

Ern and Fred were out in the open, firing at the fleeing horsemen. But the galloping targets were difficult to hit. And with every few seconds that passed, Wast and his *segundo* got further out of range.

'Kin yuh believe thet?' breathed Bandy at his side.

'That hombre must have moved quick!' snapped Jack.

'D'yuh reckon we got the other two rannies?'

'Seems like it. Wast and Tribe must ha' been quick to grab a cayuse the minute the dynamite came down. Yeah. I guess that's it. Those hombres lighted out in

136

the few seconds between seeing the sticks come down and the explosion.'

'Mighty quick work!' muttered Bandy.

'Wal, let's git down,' Jack called out determinedly. 'If we didn't kill Wast, we shore showed him we can tangle his loop!'

The decent of the canyon wall was difficult at this side, for centuries of wind had smoothed the rock as bald as an egg. But they found a channel that ran down at an angle and gave into a crack like a chimney. When Bandy and Jack climbed down to the vertical chimney, they found they could move downwards by bracing their legs and arms against the chimney walls. Slowly, and with much effort, they descended.

Finally, they reached the sandy bed of the canyon. They set off at a run for the other side. They were powdered with dust and sweat. They gave one glance at the spot which had hidden Wast and his hands. They saw two dead horses and two spreadeagled men. The men were nearly buried in rubble.

Two more of Wast's rannigans had paid the price of villainy.

Jack Griffin reached Jane as she came out to meet him. He held her arms for a moment.

'You are not hurt?' she said, searching his face.

'Nope. Everyone's all right this side, too, I guess. So Wast got away?'

'We saw him,' said Jane. 'The moment the first dynamite came down, he dashed for his horse. Otto Tribe was just as quick, but the other two men must have delayed. I – I – can't help feeling that it's terrible. I hate death! They are dead, aren't they?'

He held her arm and walked back with her to where Ern and Fred stood, still holding their rifles.

'Guess those fellers are dead all right, Jane,' he answered quietly. 'But don't waste any sympathy on 'em. Those sidewinders were only happy when gunning for some galoot.'

'Now them jiggers are buzzard bait – iffen we don't git 'em buried pretty quick!' grunted Bandy. 'Buzzards is bad luck. We don't want 'em in this canyon.'

'In that case, Bandy, yuh got a job,' said Jack gravely. 'I remember Ern packed a shovel when we came out. Figger yuh could go git it?'

He laughed at the chagrin on the old-timer's face. But Bandy went off for the shovel. He was afraid of buzzards bringing bad luck.

'Yuh did a good job, Jack!' Ern called out. 'Only wish yuh'd got them jiggers that rode away. durned if I could git a bead on 'em. Reckon this'll show Wast tuh stick tuh Bar-K Range after this.'

'It might,' returned Jack. 'But that feller ain't easily beaten.'

Ern looked determined.

'I aim tuh beat him – an' any other waddy that figgers to move in this canyon. I reckon tuh build a fence across the canyon mouth.'

'It's yore land,' said Jack.

'Yep, but don't forget, we all share in the gold.'

'Puttin' up a wire fence? Figger that'll keep strangers out?'

Ern looked thoughtful.

'Thar's bound to be some rannies git up here when they larn about the gold.'

138

Jack beckoned to Jane and Fred, and then shouted to Bandy.

'Reckon it's time we called a pow-wow,' he said.

Bandy came rolling back at the double.

'It's thisaway,' began Jack quietly. 'Ern reckons we're all pardners in this mine. I reckon we all accept that. Now Ern figgers it would be a good idea to fence the canyon mouth so as to keep out strangers. But I say this: we should all keep this gold mighty secret. We kin keep the secret for a while. Wast and his *segundo* knows thar's gold here, but I'm pretty shore they won't go around tellin' the folks in Green Coulee. An' we won't, either. We won't say a word for as long as possible. I reckon it'll come out though as soon as we begin to lodge the gold with the assayer's office in Abilene. Mighty queer how news gits around – an' yuh can bet it will git around once the assayer handles the gold.'

'So we keep the news of the gold to ourselves,' summarised Fred Spiceland.

'More than that,' said Jack. 'I vote we keep the gold hidden until we're ready to take it to the assayer. That'll give us time to git a shanty built up here and a fence across the canyon mouth.'

'I reckon we need a wire fence horse high, hog tight and bull strong,' said Ern. 'Plenty o' wire an' plenty o' posts!'

'Won't someone come along and wonder what's goin' on?' inquired Fred.

'Not many galoots git out here,' said Ern. 'An' if some ranny comes nosin' around, we kin say we're boring for water.'

Jack Griffin summed up the situation.

139

'Wal, we mine as much gold as possible before we take trail to the assayer in Abilene. an'; we button up our lips. Maybe there'll be trouble from Wast. I don't know. But I reckon thet hombre can't chase yuh off this range now that yuh know the secret, Ern.'

'He's got the cows with the worked-over brands,' June pointed out.

'We'll handle thet when it comes up,' said Jack. 'An' I reckon I've got to git back to town. I'm the sheriff, I guess. Shore would like to give yuh a hand rakin' up the gold!'

Ern slapped his back.

'Yuh done yore share when yuh an' Bandy fixed those jiggers with the dynamite. Git back to town and deal with Wast iffen he figgers to make trouble with them cows he planted on my range. An' yuh kin take Jane back to thet hotel.'

'But I want to help!' protested Jane. 'I've only another two days and then I've got to go back to my school in Abilene!'

'This ain't the place for a gal,' said Ern tersely. 'So git!'

Ern Spiceland's decision was right, because there could be no guarantee that Bertram Wast might not return in an effort to remove them from the canyon. There was gold at stake and gold stirred evil men to desperate deeds. Wast, who had wealth enough, coveted more wealth. The wealth of gold surpassed anything that land and cattle could provide. Bertram Wast evidently desired more and more power.

Jack got to the saddle of his roan as Jane climbed to her horse. Although she was disappointed, she realised it was not actually possible for her to stay out here in the gold canyon to help her brothers. She would not even have the opportunity to cook them a good meal at the ranch; for Ern, Fred and Bandy were staying in the canyon to make a start on the numerous jobs.

Jack rode out of the canyon with Jane. He liked the lithe figure she made as she sat astride the pinto. She looked pretty nice and capable. Her wide-brimmed hat was pushed back slightly, to reveal her golden hair. Her lips parted in a smile as she caught Jack watching her. He felt a sudden urge to take her in his arms, which was a strange feeling to a hard-riding hombre like himself.

They cantered the horses out of the broken country and found a trail that led by the Round-O Ranch and on towards Green Coulee. They found, too, that there was plenty to talk about. They discussed the gold, Bertram Wast and his now readily apparent villainies, and the future. Especially the future. The gold had altered everything. They did not quite realise just how much difference that fissure at the base of the canyon wall would make to their lives. Ezra Hide, the old gold-hound, had altered all their lives. There was now no pressing need to make money by ranching. Jane could leave her school – if she wanted to. But Jack had plans for Jane which would change *her* life even more than the finding of gold!

They were riding out within a few miles of the Round-O spread when Jack spied a cloud of dust a few miles to the east of them.

He guessed it was caused by a small herd of cattle

on the move. They were being driven hard. The cattle were not likely to move as fast as that if not prodded on by men. Even the leery Texas longhorn liked to take it easy unless spooked by thunder or fire.

Then Jack realised there were a number of riders herding the cattle towards Green Coulee .This was Round-O Range.

He had a sudden good hunch that it was Wast or his Bar-K hands rounding up the cattle with the altered brands.

'Guess it's Wast again, Jane,' he said. 'Now why should that feller want to drive those beefs to Green Coulee?'

'I don't know, but I'll bet he's wanting to stir up trouble,' returned Jane.

'Shore is a hard man!' murmured Jack Griffin.

He decided there was nothing to be gained by riding in close. In fact, he wanted to see Jane back to the comparative safety and comfort of the Packhorse Hotel. Green Coulee might be a Texas town, but the majority of the citizens were all for law and order. Shooting hombres was frowned on, as befitted a town that wanted to match up to the respectability of distant Abilene.

The longish ride drew to a close when the after-noon sun finally moved closer to the horizon. The sun shone its red, glaring rays into the dusty streets of the town. Jack and Jane had long ago passed the Bar-K herders.

A little weary after the day's riding, Jane went into her hotel. Jack rode along to the sheriff's office. He hitched the reins to the tie-rail and unlocked the office door.

He sat down in his quarters, and for a moment pondered the strange turn of events. If there were no hitch in the proceedings, he was now rich! All they had to do was get the gold mined. Enough could be raked out of the surface sand to last them for years!

He shook his head sadly as he thought of Ezra. Then he dismissed such thoughts from his mind. He stripped and washed the sweat and dust from his body. He donned a new red-and-black check shirt, pinned the sheriff's star to the pocket flap. He rummaged in his bag and got out a new pair of pants. They were brown and tan, and in the fashion of the day. He polished his riding boots and tucked the trousers into them. He put a green bandanna round his neck. He strapped on his gun-belts and examined his Colts. Then he was ready to eat.

He went out to eat. But first he took the roan along to the livery. The cayuse needed food and water too. Jack proceeded along to China Joe's eating-house. He ordered steak and coffee; and when he saw the rich red steak flopping over the sides of his plate, he reckoned it was better than he could dish up for himself.

It was some time later when he came out of China Joe's place. The sun was now a red orb on the horizon. He walked along the boardwalk, thumbs hitched in his belt.

He felt fine and on top of the world, but when he saw Otto Tribe walk stiffly into the Red Pine Saloon he knew there was still work for him to do.

With Ern Spiceland, he had found the answers to many questions concerning Bertram Wast. But men had been killed in the doing. It was not enough just to

143

sit back and know that they had beaten Wast to the discovery of the gold. The murders of Tom Mortimer, San Brant and Ezra must be avenged.

In retaliation, he had killed Red Holbin and Jed Slacks – not to mention the crazy Mexican Wast had hired. And he had captured Mike Capstaff, only to have the man killed unlawfully by Wast or his partners.

The way he saw it, he could not hang up his guns or quit the sheriff's office until he had brought Wast to book

He went through the batwing doors after Otto Tribe.

The man had ordered a drink and was standing alone and looking morosely round the bar. When Jack sauntered in, he froze.

Jack moved to the pine counter and jerked his head to the bartender. The man slid the whisky along and slowly wiped the counter.

Jack quietly turned and faced Otto Tribe. Jack leaned with his right arm on the counter. He could see the long scar on the man's dark, lean face.

'Yuh can tell Wast I'm a-comin' after him,' he said with a smile.

Otto Tribe faced Jack in the same manner. His movements were slow. His smile was just as fixed, but there was a vicious twist to his lips.

'Yuh welcome tuh come out to the spread any time, hombre,' he lipped.

'Figger tuh be waitin' for me?'

'Yeah. Could be. Wast ain't finished – an' neither am I. I don't like wranglers who play with dynamite!'

'Dynamite is shore hard tuh handle,' smiled Jack.

144

'Not so hard iffen you know it's coming!' leered the other.

'I want the names o' the waddies who did the branding job,' said Jack conversationally.

The leer dropped from Otto Tribes' face. His mouth tightened.

'What branding job?'

'The worked-over brands on the cows yuh were drivin' out o' the Round-O Ranch jest a few hours ago.'

Otto Tribe sneered.

'Wast has got a nice play figgered wi' them cows. He's bringin' them in to town. Gonna put 'em in the cattle corrals. Figgers tuh show the folks in this town that Spiceland is a no-good rustler. Then maybe he kin git a posse an' take the law in tuh his own hands, seein' yuh kinda partial tuh Spiceland and his sister. An' ef some git shot dead while resistin' a posse, then it'll be too bad!'

Jack tossed his whisky into the leering face. For a second the man blinked and clawed at his eyes.

Jack brought his fist back and then smashed it into the ramrod's jaw. The heavy man staggered back under the one punch. He slithered into a table and a leg cracked suddenly.

Jack Griffin followed up and crashed two more bunched fists into the swarthy face. Then the ramrod of the Bar-K lurched away and tried to draw his guns. Jack kicked one from his hand and surged in close as the other came out of leather.

He got a grip on the man's wrist, and as the gun eased out Jack jerked savagely. The gun clattered to the ground.

The other men in the bar sidled to the walls to give the combatants room. There was little comment, and there was little move to interrupt.

A fist cracked on bone. Jack staggered back. Otto Tribe had plenty of steam in his punches. Jack used the pine counter as a springboard and propelled himself at the man. He crashed into the ramrod, and they both lurched against a partition. The wood splintered and shuddered. Jack swung a slow, heavy blow into Otto Tribe's stomach. The man grimaced in agony. Jack pitched another higher up at the man's heart. Otto Tribe buckled and swung his arms at Jack, pushing him away. Jack pounded the man's face with a double right and left. The man began to lurch drunkenly, trying to get away from the partition.

Jack grabbed his shirt and held him.

'Tell me the names o' them waddies!'

'Yuh kin go tuh hell!'

A fist slammed into the ramrod's mouth and drew a spurt of blood. Jack chopped a blow at the side of the man's neck, knowing it would hurt. He felt grim. But this was the only way to deal with men of this type. He crashed his weight against Otto Tribe, keeping the man's arms pinned. With his other fist he chopped viciously at the other's neck. The man lurched drunkenly.

'I want tuh know who did the branding job. Who made the iron?'

Still the man did not answer. He tried to lurch out of Jack's reach. He shook his head to clear the fog that was paralysing his arms and legs.

Jack slammed further savage punishment into the

contorted face, and so far as Otto Tribe was concerned, the last vestige of resistance collapsed.

'I made the iron. Me and Eli White roped and branded those cows and drove 'em on to Round-O Range!'

'Nice to hear that!' panted Jack. 'Wal, I got a cell for yuh. Maybe yuh can confess a bit more when yuh git time to figger it out!'

He hustled the man to the batwing doors and then stopped.

'Did yuh fellers hear that confession?' he asked the silent customers.

There was silence while some punchers looked dubiously at each other.

'Don't rightly git what's all about,' said one.

'All right!' snapped Jack. 'I'm arrestin' this galoot for the murder o' a prospector by the name o' Ezra Hide.'

'Did he kill thet old buzzard?' asked a puncher.

'I figger to prove it soon.'

But the parley had given Otto Tribe time to clear his head and summon up new strength. With a sudden leap he was free from Jack's hands. He crashed through the batwing doors and ran over the board-walk, scattering two passers-by. He leaped for his horse tied to the hitching-rail. He was on the animal by the time Jack dashed into the street.

Jack Griffin was standing in the dusty road when Otto Tribe jabbed cruel rowels into his horse. The horse leaped forward in sudden fright, and before Jack could jump clear the animal knocked him down.

As Jack sprawled, the horse cleared him by sheer

instinct. Jack was dazed. He moved, half sat up and shook his head like a dog rescued from water.

Otto Tribe wheeled his horse, came back. He reared the animal, rowelling it wickedly. The horse's hoofs stabbed air above Jack's head – and then it came down with all its weight!

9
Wast's Last Move

It was just by a desperate twist that Jack rolled over in the dust like a curled ball, clearing the hoofs as they kicked into the road. Jack slithered away, and the Bar-K ramrod urged the horse forward and reared it up at the same time.

There was not time for Jack Griffin to get to his feet. His only movements were confined to desperate rollings and scramblings in the dust as the horse's hoofs slashed down again. By a miracle the hoofs of the frightened horse missed him. Otto Tribe was trying to kill him under the pounding hoofs!

For the third time Jack rolled clear of the plunging horse, and then, seeing that there was a split second of time given to him, he leaped to his feet.

He crouched, hands at guns. His face was set in hard, graven lines.

Otto Tribe wheeled the horse again and spurred him towards Jack. The ramrod's face was twisted with hate.

In the seconds given to him, Jack's guns whipped out and roared flame in the evening light.

There were two simultaneous explosions. Otto Tribe pitched from the saddle and hit the ground with a distinct thud. The horse slithered on its haunches with fright. Jack jumped back and almost stumbled.

The roar of gunfire brought men to the scene. As if by magic, old Doc Turner appeared.

'Another dead 'un! Goshdarn it, this town will be in debt this year owin' to burial parties!'

Jack stuck his hardware back in his holsters. He wiped the sweat from his face with the green bandanna. He stared morosely at the dead man. He had not wanted to kill him. He felt a sudden hatred of his guns. And then he felt a sudden hatred of the men who were forcing this kind of play on him.

But the man had tried to ride him down and kill him. There had been no other alternative but to shoot if he did not want to be smashed to red pulp by plunging hoofs!

'Yuh saw what happened!' Jack called to the bystanders. 'This galoot is a killer. Killed an old feller by the name o' Ezra Hide. This jigger had a pardner. I'm a-goin' to git that pardner.'

He walked slowly away in the direction of the livery.

It was fifteen minutes later when he slowly rode his horse out of Green Coulee. He wanted to stop and say goodnight to Jane, but he felt something deter him. If he told her he intended to ride out to the Bar-K she would try to stop him

150

The sun was a red ball of dying fire when he rode out and hit the trail. And almost at once he rode into the small herd of cattle coming into town. He recognised the longhorns as the over-branded cows that had been planted on Ern's range. Too, he recognised Bertram Wast astride his black horse. With him, prodding the cattle, were two other punchers. Jack did not know them.

Jack pulled into the few cottonwoods that lined the trail to Green Coulee. He had acted quickly before the others had time to recognise him. Probably they thought the rider had turned off the trail.

The cattle came on. They were lean Texas longhorns, leery and highly on the prod. Bertram was riding point, and as he cantered past the cottonwoods, Jack rode his horse out. He had a rifle ready and there was a shell in the breech. It was a repeating Remington.

'Keep yore hands high, Wast!' Jack called.

Wast turned his head, froze indecisively for a second and then slowly held his hands shoulder level. He smiled. The other two waddies at the other side of the small herd halted their horses. While they stared, Jack motioned with his rifle.

'Don't move to yore guns! That's right! Act sensible!'

Wast was still smiling.

'You can't get away with this fool play, Griffin. Why the hold-up?'

'Where d'yuh think yuh goin' with those longhorns?'

'Taking them into town. Kinda evidence. My hands

151

can testify they were found on Round-O Range.'

Jack let him have it.

'Yore sidekick, Otto Tribe, is dead!'

Bertram Wast lost his smile. His powerful, intelligent face showed a flicker of uncertainty.

'Is that so, Griffin? Who murdered him? You? Guess the folks of this town should string yuh up!'

'He asked for it, an' I shot in self-defence, if yuh must know. And yuh're the hombre who's gonna git strung up. Yuh hired an outlaw to kill Tom Mortimer and Sam Brant. Yuh're responsible for the death o' Ezra Hide, the old prospector. I aim to pin it on yuh, Wast, sooner or later. Yuh've over-played yore hand tryin' to git more wealth.'

A great struggle was going on within Bertram Wast. The outward signs were the flicker in his eyes, the twisting of his lips. He knew he was beaten, and more. He knew his neck was in danger. This hard, lean sheriff wanted justice.

'Yuh can't pin anything on me, Griffin. I deny yore accusations. You got any proof of these cockeyed stories? Yuh'd have to take me before a judge in Abilene. That judge is a friend o' mine!'

Jack breathed hard. He knew Wast played a good hand.

'Right now, yuh can git these cows drove back to yuh ranch,' he ordered. 'And I'm a-goin' with yuh.'

With the rifle as a persuading force, he rode round the herd and made the men turn the cows. Jack kept the men before him all the time. He kept his eyes on Wast principally. When the herd turned back, he rode close behind Bertram Wast.

All at once, Jack heard one puncher say to the other:

'I'll ride drag, Eli.'

Jack smiled. If Wast held a good hand, fate still played a few good cards his way! He wanted to speak to a man called Eli White. For Eli White was the man who had helped Otto Tribe to alter the brands on the cows!

Jack did not speak to the man called Eli White until they had the cows back on Bar-K Range and were nearing the Bar-K Ranch buildings. Eli White was a scraggy, medium-sized rannigan with a grey moustache and the bright, gimlet eyes of a man who was continually scheming.

Bertram Wast rode calmly, making no attempt to try trickery. Jack had glanced more than once at the man, wondering if he packed a gun. There was no sign of one. Wast wore no holster. Maybe it was his way of imitating the more civilised individuals such as judges, doctors and storekeepers, and maybe it was a trick.

For Wast had no compunction about murder. Therefore, there was no reason why he should not carry a gun.

Suddenly, Jack called a halt. The Bar-K buildings were just ahead, screened by cottonwoods.

'All right. Eli White, yuh can ride back with me,' said Jack.

The man showed surprise.

'What d'yuh want with me, Sheriff?'

'I want yuh to sign a statement back in my office.'

'I ain't signing no statement,' snarled the man, glancing uncertainly at his employer.

153

'But I reckon yuh will. I want a statement sayin' yuh helped Otto Tribe to alter the brands o' some cattle from Bar-K to Round-O and then drove the beef on to Ern Spiceland's spread. The statement will say that this scheme was part o' a plan to frame Ern Spiceland for rustling, and that the hombre who figgered it out was Bertram Wast.'

Eli White laughed uncertainly, revealing yellowed teeth beneath his moustache.

'Yuh must think I'm crazy! Shore I'll come wi' yuh, if yuh make a play wi' thet rifle. But yuh can't make me sign no statement!'

There was triumph in the man's voice. Wast exchanged glances with his hand, and they both smiled.

'Yuh'll come,' said Jack with conviction. 'An' I'll tell you why.'

'Go ahead. Spit it out!' And the man laughed.

'Yuh'll come with me an' sign the statement, *because yore life isn't worth a Mex dollar*! Yuh're dangerous to Wast because yuh know too much. I figger yuh know more about Wast than jest the branding job. I figger yuh were one o' the riders who tried to burn the Round-O Ranch-house. An' maybe yuh were one o' the waddies that made off with Jed Slack's body. Yore testimony could fix Wast proper.'

'I ain't making no statement!' snarled the man again.

He fingered his moustache nervously.

'I know yuh wouldn't cross Wast,' aid Jack steadily, 'because in the ordinary way yuh would be scared and there'd be no reward for taking risks. Wast knew that

154

when he hired yuh. But I've got plenty o' dinero tuh tempt yuh, Eli. I've got a few thousand dollars in the bank at Green Coulee. Yuh kin have the lot if yuh testify against Wast. An' remember, yuh neck ain't worth much as long as yuh within reach o' Wast. It will pay yuh to ride back with me.'

Jack paused and watched the man carefully. The reasoning was penetrating the fellow's skull. He glanced with increasing uneasiness at Bertram Wast.

Wast merely smiled.

'He's bluffing yuh, Eli,' said Wast smoothly.

The man snarled suddenly.

'Like heck he is. This needs some figgerin' out! By heck, it do!'

'Five thousand dollars for yuh if yuh kin get me evidence,' insisted Jack. 'Five thousand and a chance to hit the borders. Plenty o' places in Mexico where a hombre with five thousand dollars could fix himself up mighty fine. Stick around with Wast, feller, an' yuh'll die o' lead pisen. Yuh're too dangerous to live.'

Eli White glowered at Wast for an appreciable moment. The seeds were sprouting. But the man distrusted everybody.

'This hombre is bluffing, Eli,' snapped Wast. 'An' yuh can't jest say anythin' against me. Yuh couldn't prove anything. He knows that, Eli. Don't let him outsmart yuh!'

'He ain't,' said the man craftily. 'An' yuh ain't, neither, Mister Wast. I kin talk plenty. I was in thet firin' party when we tried tuh burn the Round-O buildings, and I kin talk about that. An' I was one o' the hands who got Jed Slacks out o' the sheriff's office.

155

I kin talk plenty. This jigger is right. Yuh're figgerin' tuh git rid o' me. Red Holbin's gone – so's Otto Tribe an' those fellers up in the canyon. Yuh want to lie quiet now. Yuh figger yuh over-played yore hand.'

'That's mighty fine reasonin',' said Jack. 'An' true. Yuh coming with me, hombre? I'm gettin' mighty sick o' holding this Remington!'

'Shore, I'm a-comin',' snapped Eli White, and he wheeled his horse.

'Shore know when yuh're backin' the wrong hand, don't yuh?' murmured Jack. 'All right, Wast, ride ahead, until yuh're outa range.'

'Yuh're not so clever,' returned Wast. 'I'll dispute that hombre's word. Yuh'll never make it stick.'

And with that he rode away, displaying a confidence which made Jack Griffin smile. But the smile was a wary one, crinkling the corner of his eyes.

Jack Griffin rode back to Green Coulee and stuck Eli White in a cell. The man protested.

'What about thet dinero? I aim tuh sign right now! An' I figger to ride out tonight!'

'Yuh'll ride out tomorrow,' said Jack sternly.

He sent a passer-by for Doc Turner, Joe Blade and the manager of the Packhorse Hotel. They were all reputable men in the town, and would make good witnesses.

'I'm signin' yuh in as deputies for the night,' said Jack.

'Where's that durned deputy o' yours?' inquired Doc Turner.

'He's kinda busy.'

Jack led them to the boardwalk outside the office,

and he lit a kerosene lantern that hung there.

'I want plenty o' people tuh see us,' he said strangely. 'Stand here for a bit. Then we go over to yore hotel, Mister Gorman.'

He would not explain. After loafing on the board-walk for nearly fifteen minutes, they strolled over to the Packhorse Hotel. The street was fairly well lighted by lanterns, and the four men could be observed entering the hotel.

Jack led them to the rear of the hotel, and they went out a back door. They stood in the gloom of the back alleys.

'We're goin' back to the office, an' we're takin' a route round by the dark alleys,' instructed Jack.

There was some grumbling by Doc Turner, but they moved quietly round the main street, crossing higher up in a gloomy part and then returning to the sheriff's office by way of the back alleys. There were no lights. Jack had a key to the back door of the office. This door had hardly been used.

The door gave on to a passage which ran to the office housing the cell containing Eli White. In the passage was a large locker which was a kind of store. It could accommodate four men. And Jack ordered them to get inside.

'Iffen I'm wrong, gents, I'll apologise, but I got a hunch we'll git a visitor. A certain hombre may think I'm in the Packhorse with you gents.'

If he was right in his hunch, Jack knew he would not have long to wait. For the certain hombre would figure that the chance this presented might not last for long.

For fully ten minutes Jack and the other men waited with grim, tense curiosity. Then a key scraped in the front door at the other end of the passage. The scraping continued for sometime, as though the key were not the right type. Finally, the door opened. A tall man walked quietly and confidently along the passage to the office.

Jack peered through the slit made by the partially closed door, and knew the man was Bertram Wast.

Wast went into the office.

Jack stepped out, hitched his hands near his guns. He had a taut, flat feeling inside.

A man's voice cursed and screamed.

'No! Yuh skunk, Wast. Don't shoot!'

Eli White was shouting for his life.

Jack stepped into the office.

'Wast!' he called softly.

The big man in the black suit turned with the soft, lithe speed of a mountain lion.

There was a a little derringer in Wast's hand. The dull-plated little gun barked, and Jack felt a red-hot pain stab his chest.

He squeezed the trigger of his own gun. As the little derringer barked again, a Colt slug bore into Wast's heart. Jack put out one hand and grimaced with pain. He swayed. He saw the unbelievable. Wast was still standing on his feet, a contorted grin on his face. A patch of red welled round his vest. The man raised the tiny gun with a dreadfully slow movement.

Jack stared with dazed eyes. He felt incapable of aiming his gun.

And then, with a horrible gasp, Bertram Wast slowly

pitched sideways and lay still on the wooden floor.

'I figgered – he'd – try tuh – kill Eli White!' panted Jack. 'I couldn't git him any other way. Gunsmoke shore took charge o' – the other hombres – who – might ha' – given evidence agin him—'

And then Jack passed out and went into a pit of darkness.

A few days later he was in bed, sitting up and looking pretty cheerful. Jane had just entered the room, and Doc Turner was going.

'Guess you'll patch up pretty good,' cackled the old man. 'Can't do that for Wast. That feller Eli White spilled the beans. Got another waddy to testify that Wast hired Mike Capstaff to kill Tom Mortimer. Seems this waddy knew more'n Wast figured. Are you going to give Eli White his money?'

'Give the rat the money,' said Jack quietly. 'It won't do him any good, I reckon. It was gold that urged Wast on to his doom. He got so tangled, he overplayed his hand. An' that hombre had enough money for any feller.'

Doc Turner waved and ambled out.

Jack stared appreciatively at Jane. She was wearing her best dress.

'Yuh look prettier that way than in blue Jeans and shirt,' he gulped. 'Though I kinda like yuh in them, too, Jane.'

'Do you just like – like – me?' she wanted to know.

'Goshdarn it – no! I love you, Jane! Can yuh be the wife of a gold-mine owner – or would you figure on being a rancher's wife?'

She smoothed his pillow, and then suddenly placed her lips to his. He placed one arm round her shoulders and then, suddenly, he held her tightly with two hands.

A full minute later she said:

'I don't care whether it's gold or cattle – as long as I'm your wife. Oh, Jack, I only want you better, never mind gold or cattle!'

He nodded his head in admiration.

'That's what I'm a-hangin' up my guns for!'

X